# MERIDIAN SIX

JAYE WELLS

Meridian Six



ISBN: 1494746875
ISBN-13: 978-1494746872

# OTHER BOOKS BY JAYE WELLS

**The Prospero's War Series**
Dirty Magic
Cursed Moon (August 2014)
Deadly Spells (2015)

**The Sabina Kane Series**
Red-Headed Stepchild
The Mage In Black
Green-Eyed Demon
Silver-Tongued Devil
Blue-Blooded Vamp
Violet Tendencies (short story)
Rusted Veins (novella)

# A LETTER TO READERS

This novella was originally a short story, titled "Red Life." In fact, it was the first story I ever got published. It appeared in the Weirdly II: Eldritch anthology from Wild Child publishing. The story was short—too short—and I always wanted to go back and explore more of this dark world.

Be warned: There are no snarky sidekicks or hilarious hijinks in this story. Instead, there are horrors and heartaches in Meridian Six's bleak world. But there is also hope. Something we can all use a little more of in our own world.

I wish you happy reading.

Jaye Wells
May 2013

# ONE.

The frigid air scraped my lungs raw. I pumped my legs faster, praying for a second wind. Stopping wasn't an option. Their breath beat at my back, and if they caught me, I'd be dead.

I turned the corner, running down an alley. Footsteps echoed behind me. Faster. I wrenched two trashcans back into their path. A male cursed and grunted. Metal scraped against concrete. I focused on the mouth of the alley and prayed for a miracle.

A black sedan screeched to a stop in front of me. I didn't hesitate. My legs ached with the exertion, but I just managed to launch myself onto the hood. On the other side, the landing lurched every joint in my body.

*Keep running. Find the light. Red means life.*

Behind me, deep voices argued. I continued

down the street, cursing the heels the Castor had forced me to wear for the Prime's birthday celebration. I couldn't spare the precious moments to rid myself of the torture devices.

Finally, a speck of red appeared in the distance. All thoughts of sore feet and desperation evaporated. The beckoning light glowed from the porch of a squat, run-down house that looked more like a prewar crack den than a haven for the lost.

I kicked up my pace and pushed through the pain. Salvation drew closer.

My pursuers' harsh breathing echoed off the burnt out shells of buildings and trash- strewn streets. A weathered poster bearing my own face mocked me from the brick walls of an old induction center. In red ink along the bottom, the Troika's slogan, the hated words I'd repeated so often on radio broadcasts and in speeches to grim-faced prisoners: "Blood will make you free."

Not a soul lurked in the shadows. Most humans now slaved in work camps or blood camps. Rebels sought refuge in the burnt-out cities, but if any were watching me from the darkened windows, their survival instincts precluded them from interfering in Troika business. After all, my pursuers wore the telltale black uniforms of the secret police. The lightning symbol on their breasts had become a graphic promise of pain.

Not far now. If I could just—

Pain exploded on my scalp. My head whipped back with the force of the fist jerking back on the ponytail. My feet snapped out from under me. He used my hair to keep me from hitting the ground. The agony made me wish I'd hit concrete instead.

It was Sergei, one of the Prime's personal guards, who'd caught me. The one who always watched me while caressing his precious riding crop. "Got you, bitch." His eyes burned like hot coals. Fangs flashed as he panted for breath. "Now we can add evading arrest to your list of crimes."

His partner doubled over, trying to catch his breath. I didn't know his name, but he had the wild eyes of a male who enjoyed his job too much. He glanced up at the glowing red light on the front of the house, now only twenty feet away. "She almost made it."

"Almost doesn't count," Sergei said, tugging my hair harder. He leaned in at my grimace. "You like that?" he whispered. "There's more coming." I gritted my teeth and waited for my opportunity. "Call headquarters and have them send a rover to retrieve her."

With the partner distracted, I slapped his fist to my scalp, holding it in place and easing the pressure. I scraped my heel down his shin and stabbed the tip into his foot. With a yelp, he released me. I grabbed the crop from his slack hold and jerked it against his windpipe.

It happened so fast his friend didn't see it. He

spoke into his radio, his back to me, "Repeat: Meridian Six has been subdued—" I grabbed the blade from my garter and made his last words dissolve into a wet gurgle. As he fell, I grabbed his gun from his hand and turned it on Sergei.

"You won't be allowed to live." His words the confidence of a man determined to deliver the deathblow. "You'd already be dead if Director Castor didn't want the pleasure for himself."

I put the gun to his head. Pulled the trigger. His body jerked. Wetness splashed my face. I dropped his body and hauled ass toward the steps.

It happened as if in slow motion. I ran toward the door, my hand rose to pound. The roar and vibration of the Troika's arriving craft shook the building. The panel in front of me flew open. A female in red robes opened her mouth in shock, reaching for me. The blast ripped through the night. Fire exploded in my left shoulder. I fell in slow motion, the world a blur of pain—fell across the threshold and into the acolyte's arms. Blood filled my vision.

*Red means life.*

# TWO.

Whispers woke me. I peeled open one eye. Two females watched me from the doorway. I didn't move so as not to alert them to my newly conscious state. Not until I had a chance to take stock.

Drab-colored clothes were folded in a neat pile on the chair by the door. The stained and ripped green silk dress I'd been wearing hung from a hook and the high heels lay beneath them on the floor like two drunks. Across from the bed, a canvas hung depicting the beatified visage of some patron saint of the Sanguinarians, the religion to which the Order of the Sisters of Crimson belonged. On the table beneath the painting, lay the dagger I'd stolen off the guard when I'd made my escape. When I'd arrived it was bloody, but now it shone like pristine, polished silver.

A thin, coarse blanket abraded my naked skin. The realization that I was totally at the mercy of these bloodthirsty holy women shocked my synapses into firing again.

*They call me Meridian Six*

"She is awake." The voice was feminine with an undercurrent of steel.

*I used to be a tool for the Troika. But now I am their prey.*

Turning my head, I focused on the pair by the door. The acolyte who'd helped me inside earlier stood next to a statuesque woman in crimson and black robes. All Sisters of Crimson wore red robes, but only those who'd achieved exalted status wore the sacred black as well.

*Chatelaine...smart not to leave an acolyte alone with me. Not after the way I arrived.*

She dismissed the acolyte with a nod. The door closed, and she moved forward slowly, almost gliding. She wasn't afraid to be alone with me.

"Welcome. I am Sister Agrippa, Chatelaine of this rectory."

She shushed me and placed a hand on my arm when I tried to sit up. "You must rest. The bullet grazed your shoulder, but you lost blood from your other wounds."

I didn't meet her eyes and pulled the sheet higher. She'd seen the bite marks on my thighs and breasts.

"What happened to your lower back?"

I looked up quickly, thankful she hadn't mentioned the other wounds. "Had to dig out the chip so they couldn't zap me."

She nodded but showed no emotion on her face. "You wouldn't have made it far if you hadn't." Something lit in her eyes—respect? "It's a miracle you made it out of the Fortress as it is, Miss Six."

I fell back onto the flat pillow. Even my bones felt exhausted. I wasn't surprised Sister Agrippa knew the name the vamps had given me. Everyone knew about Meridian Six, model Troika citizen. The instant I escaped I swore I'd never be called that name again, but I didn't want to offend the holy woman when the situation was still so fragile. "Thanks," I said instead.

She eyed me with frank curiosity. "I assume you are aware I am only able to offer you sanctuary for twenty-four hours. You slept twenty of those away, I'm afraid."

I cringed. Four hours wasn't much time. I needed to regroup and come up with a plan. "I understand, Sister. I appreciate your hospitality."

"I took the liberty of having my assistant bring a change of clothes." She nodded at a stack of garments on a chair next to the door. "I guessed at your size, but they'll be better than the filthy ones you wore when you arrived." Her face didn't betray any judgment but I found her choice of adjective telling. Had my harlot's clothes and the blood kiss marks on my inner thighs and chest betrayed my status as the Troika's blood whore?

I wasn't sure how to reply. Thanking her again would have felt too much like a confession.

"I'll leave you to your ablutions. The first mass of the evening begins in five minutes. Perhaps you'll join us? Spiritual renewal may offer you a modicum of strength for your journey."

"I think I'll pass." I hesitated before adding, "No offense."

"None taken. I didn't think you'd agree anyway." She moved to the door again. "Go ahead and get dressed. I'll have my assistant retrieve you after mass, and we can discuss next steps."

"Sister?"

"Hmm?" She paused by the door. The brighter light from the hallways fell around her like a halo.

"Aren't you going to ask why the Troika are after me?"

She paused and smiled, her small, white fangs flashing in the dim light. "Would you tell me the truth if I did?"

My lips quirked. I liked this woman's straightforward, no-bullshit attitude. "Probably not."

She nodded and left, closing the door behind her. I sat in silence for a few more moments, trying to will myself out of the warm cocoon of the bed. My soul ached to stay in this quiet place. My body ached for stillness. But my mind wasn't having any of that. I needed a plan—and fast. I'd have a lot more than aches to worry about if the Troika's men caught me when I left the convent.

Twenty minutes later, I'd completed my fortieth lap of the small room in the foreign-feeling clothes. The coarse woolen sweater and baggy denim weren't exactly the quality I was used to. I normally opted for simple garments of the highest caliber fabrics that wouldn't hamper movement or snag. Castor insisted that my clothes should also show off my form to its best advantage, which was why I didn't mind the shapeless garments the sisters provided. And the shoes! The soft leather moccasins hugged my feet like a dream. They'd be a hell of a lot easier to run in than the heels the Director of Propaganda insisted I wear.

His face flashed in my mind's eye. The lascivious gleam when he'd presented me with the dress and shoes. "And don't forget the hairpiece," he'd said, waving the green silk ribbon. "All birthday gifts should be topped with a bow." He'd giggled and left muttering to himself about how clever he was for thinking of the perfect birthday gift for the Prime.

Me.

A soft knock on the door announced the acolyte's return. "The Chatelaine will see you now."

I nodded and followed her out into the corridor. I'd considered wandering around earlier while I waited, but I didn't want to be rude. The corridor's ceilings hung low over sconces lining the walls, giving off a warm glow. Funny, from the outside this building seemed condemned, but inside it was clean and peaceful.

"Are we below ground?" I asked, noting the lack of windows.

She nodded meekly over her shoulder.

I waited for more information, but she didn't offer any. The sisters, I guessed, probably built this sanctuary in abandoned tunnels dug during the Blood Wars. I'd heard how the humans and vampire rebels had dug warrens under the cities for quick escapes during skirmishes. Now, the dirt walls had been plastered over, but the echoes of old fear clung to the air like the musk of turned earth.

We reached a door, and the acolyte knocked. "The Chatelaine is waiting."

"Thank you, Sister—"I let the word hang there for her to fill in.

She avoided my eyes and scuttled off. Her red robes swirled around her ankles as she rounded the corner. I wondered briefly how she ended up living in abandoned tunnels below the city, offering succor to fugitives like me.

"Six?" The Chatelaine's voice pulled me out of my musings. I took a deep breath, raised my chin and marched into her inner sanctum.

She sat behind a battered wooden desk. A single low-watt bulb hung from the ceiling. The threadbare tapestries stretched across sections of the walls did nothing to dispel the chill. One depicted a unicorn bleeding in a cage and another a knight fighting a dragon.

"Nice," I said, more to get the conversation going than out of any real appreciation for the artistry.

"Functional," she countered. "They help insulate against the dankness."

I took the seat she offered. The ancient metal chair creaked in protest. I cringed as the sound echoed through the cave-like room.

The Chatelaine stared into a vid-screen, an alien bit of technology for such an ascetic setting, but, then, she was a vampire. And vampires loved their tech.

I couldn't see what she was looking at, but whatever it was, she found it damned interesting. Warning bells went off in my head. Noticing my sudden stiffness, she turned the screen toward me.

My own face stared back at me. My stomach fell as I read the ticker beneath the old photo. "Fugitive still at large. The Troika is offering a reward of ten thousand charns for her capture—dead or alive."

"Meridian Six, age twenty-three, daughter of rebel sympathizer, Alexis Sargosa," she read, her brows rising. "Wanted for violation of Troika code 439."

My stomach churned, and my hands grew

damp. Given the conditions of the rectory, it was possible the Chatelaine was mentally tabulating the repairs she could make with that kind of reward.

I lifted my chin, waiting for her to make the next move.

"Code 439?" she said. "That's assault, correct?"

I gave a jerky nod to confirm that was, indeed, the crime assigned to Code 439, but I didn't feel the need to confess my innocence. After all, if things had gone as planned the charge would have been murder instead.

The nun's eyes took on a speculative gleam. My fingers slid down my leg toward the shard of metal I'd strapped to my ankle using a bit of bandage the nuns had left in my room. They'd been smart not to leave me with any glass or cutlery, but the metal bracket had torn away from the bed frame easily and its sharp corners could inflict some pain.

"Keep your weapon where it is, child. The Sisters of Crimson are no friends of the Troika, no matter how well they pay."

I paused and looked at her. "Ten thousand Cs would buy a lot of food for your acolytes, sister."

"True, but then I would have a debt on my soul I'm not prepared to repay."

"If you knew all of this I'm surprised you let me in here to begin with. Some consider me quite dangerous."

Her lips lifted in a slight smile. "Especially the

Troika."

"What makes you say that?"

"Ten thousand charns seems a bit steep for assault," she said, leaning back in her chair. "No, I think they want you for another reason."

I looked down. How much should I tell her? Even if I knew I could trust her, I'd be risking her life by sharing information she shouldn't know.

"Let's just say I have intimate knowledge of a few skeletons in the Troika's closet," I said.

"Oh, I bet you do." Her lips twitched. "So they made up the code violation then?"

"Not necessarily." I didn't elaborate. I crossed my arms to let her know that was all I had to say about the matter.

"Fair enough," she said. "I suppose you've already guessed that a crowd of Troika guards have gathered outside?"

"I figured as much."

"You got a plan?"

"Run like hell."

"In other words, you've got no plan at all." She leaned forward with her elbows on the desk. If she hadn't been wearing the robes of a holy order, her expression would have reminded me of a conspirator. "Lucky for you, I do."

# THREE.

The Chatelaine walked ahead of me down a musty corridor hidden behind one of the tapestries in her office.

"Are you sure the Troika doesn't know about these tunnels?" I asked.

"The Troika's influence ends at my door. They may control everyone else, but they're too superstitious to screw with the keepers of the sacred knowledge."

"You sure don't talk like a religious leader."

She turned to look at me, a wicked smile on her face. "I wasn't always a Sister of Crimson. It was only after the war killed my family that I took the blood vows. Before that, I led a somewhat more ... dissolute existence."

"Like what?"

"Even the holy have secrets, child." She

winked and held the torch higher. "Things get tight through here. Watch your head."

We walked a bit farther in silence. But I had questions and if I didn't ask them now, I might not have a chance. "Aren't you worried about what will happen when I don't walk out by the deadline?"

"The twenty-four hour thing is more of a self-imposed rule. Our leaders instated it when some of our guests began overstaying their welcome. The Troika has no say in our laws, so long as we continue to absolve them of their sins they leave us alone."

"Why are you helping me?"

She stopped and turned awkwardly in the narrow space. "Look, don't misunderstand. I'm not in the business of liberating all fugitives who seek our aid. My priority is protecting my Sanguinary and my acolytes. If you have information that can hurt the Troika, I'm damned well going to help you get it out there. Many of us want things to return like they were before the Troika took over."

"How do you know I'm not lying about having information on them?"

She looked me in the eyes, and an emotion I couldn't name overcame me. Something unfamiliar, yet powerful. I couldn't put my finger on it.

"Don't let my coarse talk and practical manner fool you, child. I am a believer. And I believe the goddess put you on my doorstep for a reason. It is not my place to question this. It is my duty to follow my gut and further Her plans." The light in her eyes suddenly made sense to me.

Sister Agrippa had faith.

I only believed in three things: my right fist, my left fist, and my gut. The vein of mysticism running through the Troika's top echelons made me uneasy. But if the sister's belief in the divine was the reason she was helping me, I wasn't going to refuse.

"Besides," she continued, "I knew your mother." She walked ahead, leaving me slack-jawed. I sped to catch up.

"You did?"

The Chatelaine cleared a cobweb that spanned the width of the tunnel. "Long ago. Before the wars."

"How?" I asked, impatient.

"We met at school. She was one of the few Sapiens to be decent to the fanged kids when we were integrated into human schools. After graduation we lost touch. I heard she met your father and got involved in the One Species movement while I went on to ... other things." She looked off into the shadows of the tunnel, as if it was a portal to the past. "Alexis didn't have blood in her veins—she had fire. "

The admiration in Agrippa's tone made my skin feel too tight.

"I heard she passed away during the battle of

New York," the sister said after a few moments of tense silence. "I was sorry to hear that. Anyone ever tell you that you could be her twin?"

I swallowed hard against the unwanted rush of emotion rising in my throat and shook my head. The Troika hadn't been real interested in reminiscing about my mother.

She glanced at me sharply, like she wanted to interrogate me about my upbringing, but we'd reached the end of the corridor. "We're here." She pointed to a red door set in the dirt wall.

*Red means life.*

She knocked once, twice, a pause, twice more. Obviously a code. A panel slid back in the door, and two eyes peered out. "Password?" The voice sounded female, but husky enough that it might have been male.

The Chatelaine leaned forward and whispered something I couldn't hear. The door opened almost immediately.

Over the sister's shoulder, I got the impression of shadows milling around the dim space. The scent of unwashed bodies punched me in the nose.

The sister turned to me. "I must leave you here. They'll take care of you."

"What? You can't—I have no idea who these people are."

"They're friends. Members of the resistance."

"Who've you brought us, Chatelaine?" The male voice had the sharp-edged confidence of one used to being answered.

The light was so dim, I couldn't make out his face except for the outline of long hair and the stock of a shotgun jutting over his shoulder.

"This is Carmina, daughter of Alexis Sargosa." I glanced sharply at the nun. This was a fine time to finally start using my real name. "The Troika call her Meridian Six."

The man came forward into the light of the Chatelaine's torch. When his features came into view, I gasped and stumbled back into the nun. Scars webbed across his face like a mask of wax. His ruined mouth twisted into what I guessed was supposed to be a scowl. "So you're the infamous traitor?" He sniffed and jerked away like he'd smelled something foul on me. "The Troika's whore."

"Icarus." Each of the three syllables were weighed down with censure from the Chatelaine. "She's a *fugitive*. And she has information that could help the cause."

A female stepped forward. Her thin frame contradicted the posture of a warrior. Brown stubble sprouted from her pale scalp. A piercing yellow vampire's gaze raked over my body. "Bullshit. She's a Troika spy."

Sister Agrippa sighed. "No she isn't, Dare. Bringing her here was my idea."

"She just wants you to think that!" the female named Dare spat back.

"If the Troika wanted to use me to defeat the

rebels," I shot a pointed look at her threadbare clothes, "don't you think they'd send me to infiltrate one that posed an actual threat?"

She gasped and Icarus's eyes narrowed to sharp slits. Besides me, the nun muttered a curse under her breath. I should have regretted my words, which had been motivated by anger more than logic. But didn't. It sounded a lot like Agrippa wanted me to team up with the rebels, but my only plan was to get as far from the Troika as possible. I braced myself for the return attack, hoping the Chatelaine would step in should it get out of hand. Instead, after a couple of tense seconds, the vamp's lips twitched and a snort escaped her pale lips.

"Fuck you, Traitor."

"Fuck you too, Hemo," I said using the slang humans used for vampires.

Icarus kept his eyes on me while I argued with his second in command. His gaze was assessing, weighing and judging. He found me lacking if the angry twist to his lip was any indication. I met his gaze with an unblinking glare. Finally, he spit on the dirt next to my feet. "She can stay."

The air escaped the room. Sister Agrippa looked as shocked at Dare.

"Icarus—" his vampire friend began, but he shook his head and disappeared back into the room. Over his shoulder he said, "If she steps out of line, we'll just kill her."

As he walked away, I noticed his hair was long

enough to cover the back of his neck. Every human captured or born since the Troika took over was blood-typed upon birth and tattooed with their type on the back of their neck. Therefore, all humans under Troika control were required to keep their hair short or shaved completely.

My hair was short because of the regulations, but the back of my neck didn't bear the mark of my blood type. The Troika decided it would look bad on camera. Thank goodness, too, because the AB negative tattoo would be like a bull's eye to any vamp I ran into on the outside.

The vampire and I stared at each other across the threshold. My fingers itched to grab the knife at my ankle, but judging from her haggard appearance she was two seconds from flying into a blood rage. If it came to that I'd be dinner.

"Let me guess, your friends from Camp Vamp call you *Six*, right, tough girl?" the vampire said with an eye-roll.

"I don't have any friends." Especially none from "Camp Vamp" as she had so charmingly called the barracks masquerading as a school for Troika youth I'd grown up in. "And call me Carmina."

"Carmina, sure. You heard Icarus. You want to keep breathing? You'll do what we say."

I flicked an angry glance at the Chatelaine for bringing me here in the first place. Grabbing her sleeve, I pulled her a little further down the corridor. "Thanks a lot."

She shrugged. "It's either them or take your chances sneaking past the army waiting for you topside."

"Why did you tell them I have intel?"

"Well you do, don't you?"

"Sure, but I'm not interested in joining the resistance."

The older woman crossed her arms and gave me a schoolmarm glare. "You didn't have a plan at all when you ran, did you?"

I chewed my bottom lip. "My only goal was to get away from the Troika and find this place. Figured the rest would sort itself out."

Her eyes narrowed. "I'm going to give you a little bit of advice that might extend your life a little. No one makes it very far in this world without choosing a side."

I snorted. "Don't you think that's a little hypocritical coming from a woman who poses as a religious leader for the Troika while secretly supporting the rebels."

"I said you've got to pick a side, not that you had to announce it." Her lips twitched. "My point is no one can survive the Bad Lands alone. I could give you a few rations and supplies, but you wouldn't make it out there two days before a rover tracked you down or a pack of dogs caught your scent."

Seeing my hesitation, she continued. "I'm not going to force you to give me your reasons for choosing now to run, but I assume they must have been pretty good." I looked up to see sympathy in her gaze. She hadn't survived this long without knowing a thing or two about the sorts of things that made a girl finally take her chances between running and death. "But these people here? They fight on the side of freedom. And judging from what you said, freedom's what you want."

I took a deep breath as the truth of her words battered some of my resistance. When I'd formed my plan to escape, my only goal had been to find Sister Agrippa's convent. But now I had stumbled back into a rebellion that left me behind a little less than two decades earlier. A rebellion that didn't fit into my plans at all. But now it seemed that pretending to continue my mother's work was the only way to ensure my survival for the immediate future.

"The resistance is poor, underfed and outnumbered," she said. "But we're also mad as hell and we want our world back. If you have information that can help that happen, then use it to ensure you get the freedom you want."

I looked into the shadows of the tunnel behind me and thought about the secret police gathered on the Chatelaine's doorstep. I thought about my mother, who'd died fighting against the vampires who'd raised me to be the poster child for obedient humans. And I thought about how those bite marks found their way onto my thighs.

About the blood-smeared smile on the Prime's face when he told me his plans for the future. My stomach cramped with the memory of pain, of blood loss.

"Well?" Dare called from the doorway. "What's it going to be?" Icarus had come back to join her. He shot me a look that looked a lot like he expected me to lose my nerve and run.

I licked my dry lips and looked him in the eyes. "I'm in."

He laughed. "Not so fast. You'll have to pass inspection by Saga first."

"Who's Saga?"

"He's an elder of the movement," Dare offered. "If you're lying he'll know it. Regardless he'll award us rations for bringing the famous Troika Whore to him."

She was trying to get a rise out of me. I met her challenging gaze levelly. "You have me at a disadvantage it seems. After all, you know so much about me, but I've never even heard of you."

Something flickered in Icarus's eyes. He banked the fire quickly, but I'd already filed the vulnerability away in my arsenal.

"We can't leave to meet Saga until daybreak," he snapped. "It'll be a two-day walk. On the way you'll be expected to contribute to food and water stores. You threaten any of my people, you so much as look at one of them the wrong way and I don't care who the fuck your mother was, I'll end you with my bare hands."

"And do I receive the same rights should one of your people threaten me?"

"No," he said simply. "But you're welcome to go back to the Fortress if you're concerned about your safety. From the looks of you—" his gaze scraped down my frame—"you were well taken care of there."

The insult flashed like neon. To these half-starved rebels my healthy color and lack of protruding ribs were the hallmarks of a traitor. I'd never convince them I wasn't a willing blood mate to the Troika's inner circle.

"Fair enough." I held out my hand to shake on it. Icarus offered his left hand. It was then that I noticed how his right arm was atrophied and curled up against his side like a broken wing. Still, his handclasp was strong and confident, like a man who didn't let a few injuries get in the way of his strength.

"Now that that's settled," the Chatelaine stepped forward. "I've brought along a pint of blood for you, Dare, and some milk for Rabbit. I'm afraid it's all I could spare."

The vampire smiled for the first time since we arrived. Where her fangs should have been there were two empty spaces. I gasped, realizing she was a eunuch. "Were you a servant?" I blurted.

Dare froze and raised her chin. "I'm no one's slave, whore." She ran her tongue over the twin voids. "I removed them myself."

My mouth fell open. "Why?"

"Because fangs are symbols of corruption and greed."

"But without them you can't heal as fast or live as—"

"The strength I lost is offset by being able to stand proudly in the sun with my human comrades."

I had no idea how to respond to the fervor in her tone. I'd known many vampire servants over the years who'd had their fangs forcibly removed to keep them weaker than their masters. The idea of someone doing that to themselves was unfathomable.

Dismissing me, Dare bowed and kissed the Chatelaine's fingers before taking the gifts from her. "Thank you, Sister." She tossed the small bladder of milk at a lanky boy—the one the Chatelaine called "Rabbit"— who looked no older than twelve. He had a mop of black hair on his head and was so thin, his collarbones jutted from his chest like twin blades. He shot the Sister a dimpled grin that lit up the dark room and scuttled away into the corner with Dare to feast on the meager buffet.

"I must be off now," the sister said. "Six—" At my frown, she corrected herself "—I mean, Carmina ... it's been a pleasure." She pressed something into my hand.

I uncurled my fingers and looked down at the red disk with a black lotus in the center—the symbol of the Sisterhood.

"For luck," she whispered with a flash of a dimple.

I watched her walk away with a sense of dread and shock. How had all this happened so fast?

"Well?" Icarus said. He held his good hand toward the door. "You coming in?"

I looked at the red door and remembered the last words my mother said to me as the Troika army closed in. *Never stop fighting, Carmina. Red means life.*

She'd whispered them to me two seconds before the bullet slammed into her chest.

Her eyes had gone wide. "RUN!"

At the time, she'd been warning me to find one of the Sister of Crimson's convents before the Troika found me. But it had been too late for both of us back then. My mother died on her way to the Fortress for questioning, and I'd been captured before I'd stumbled tear-blinded and terrified from the burnt out shell of a building in Old New York.

In the seventeen years since that bloody night, my mother's face, her scent had blurred and disappeared from my memory. But not her voice.

I'd been raised by my mother's enemies. Trained to serve vampires. To be the model human. To spread the Troika's gospel of blood and glory. To be their whore.

Icarus raised his eyebrow in challenge when I hesitated on the threshold. I blew out a breath, placed the Chatelaine's good luck totem around my neck, and put one foot in front of the other. Dare closed the red door behind me. My heart hammered in time with the bolts slamming home.

*Red means life.*

# FOUR.

**D**awn. I couldn't remember the last time I'd seen a sunrise. After years living among the vampires, I'd forgotten the sting to the corneas, the warmth on my face, the way sunlight made the world explode in a riot of color.

Streaks of pink and yellow slashed across the horizon. But closer to our small band, the colors were deep purples and blues. Branches arched like charred bones overhead. Occasionally a puff of white steam emerged from one of our yawning mouths.

I huddled into the threadbare cloak I'd been issued. The shoes the Chatelaine had given me the night before weren't so comfortable when tested by the rocks and crags of what remained of the old highway. Back in the day, the highway had been the main artery into the city, but now it was nothing more than rubble overgrown with thick vines and the carcasses of dead trees.

This was our second day on the road. I'd spent the first day trying to keep my head down and listen to the hushed conversations of my companions. No one spoke to me, but they accepted my presence—almost like I was a dog they tolerated instead of a person.

That suited me just fine. Gave me time to think about what had happened and plan for what was coming. According to the stories Dare told Rabbit to keep him entertained, Saga was a legend among the rebels. In the before times, back when humans ran things, there had been these buildings called "libraries," which were filled with books people could borrow for free. Apparently Saga used to be in charge of one of these libraries.

Now he led an army of starving children.

"Yo, Six," Rabbit called.

I looked behind me to see him jogging to catch up with me. My steps slowed to accommodate him.

When he reached me, his breath puffed out in small clouds of white. A voice cleared nearby and I looked up to see Dare glaring at the boy for speaking to me. I ignored her and smiled at the kid.

"Is it true you're AB neg?"

I tripped over my feet as much from the shock as the thick vine that seemed to come out of nowhere. "Who told you that?"

Rabbit jerked his head toward Dare, who was suddenly very interested in her shoes.

"So what if I am?" I said, evading.

His dirty face morphed into mask of disbelief. "You're kidding, right? There's people give their right arm to be in that blood group."

And many had given their arms. Their heads and lives, too. The caste system set up by the Troika based on blood types had given humans an excuse to turn on each other in all sorts of horrible ways.

"No, Rabbit," I lied. "I'm not AB neg. The Troika made that up as part of their propaganda campaign." I wasn't lying out of some urge to be humble. I lied to save my life. Dare wasn't a Troika vamp, but I didn't trust anyone who craved blood with the knowledge that the rarest of all blood types flowed through my veins.

His face fell. "Well what are ya?"

I briefly considered saying something else, like O positive. No vampire would even think about helping themselves to my blood, then. But it also would have sent up warning bells. O positive people were the lowest of the low in the blood caste system. No doubt it would have marked me as untouchable, but it also would have raised questions since the Troika would never keep such a low-ranking human in such a public role.

"B positive," I said instead. Middle of the road. Neither coveted, nor disdained.

The kid screwed up his lips. "That's boring."

"Sorry." I shrugged. "So, is Icarus your dad or something?"

He shot me a look that said he doubted my intelligence.

I frowned at him. "Where's your family, then?"

"Mom and dad were rebels but died of the thirst when I was tiny. Dare found me and took me in." He turned and motioned at the prickly vampire who stalked down the road like she was looking for a fight.

"How did you two end up with him?" Icarus wasn't around or I wouldn't have asked. He'd spent most of the last day walking ahead to make sure the path was clear, which was fine with me.

Rabbit looked around, like he was afraid of being overheard, too. "We found him a couple years ago. Just after he escaped a labor camp,"

My brows shot up. Most humans who weren't kept as pets by the Troika were divided into labor camps and blood camps, depending on their blood types.

As far as I knew, no one escaped the camps. Ever. Of course, I got all my information from the Troika, who wouldn't be too eager to share that humans were slipping past their security on a regular basis. Still, I assumed that if Rabbit was telling the truth, Icarus had managed a feat few other humans had managed.

The boy leaned in to share secrets. "That's why he's the way he is." The boy waved a small hand over his arm to indicate Icarus's wounds. "He fell from the wall and broke his arm in five places."

"How did he get the burns?" I asked, unable to resist my curiosity.

"Oh, that was different—"

"Enough talking," Dare snapped. "We need to keep an eye out for rovers."

Rabbit shot me an apologetic look and broke away to continue his patrol of the brush around the road. As the smallest of the group, it was easiest for him to roam in the high grasses.

I glanced at Dare as the kid disappeared. She glared at me like I'd committed some huge sin of impropriety.

"Until Saga clears you, keep to yourself. I won't have you poisoning the kid with your lies."

I clenched my teeth together to keep from taking her bait. Part of me wondered if she wanted me to lose my temper and fight her. What was the point? We both knew she'd win. While I'd had some training and could hold my own, I couldn't begin to compete with the battle-honed reflexes of a vampire who'd spent most of her life scraping an existence out of the shit mountain the world had become.

"Maybe you should be telling that to the kid, then."

"You're smart, huh? We'll see what Saga says about that."

After that, we fell into silence and I focused on putting one foot in front of the other. My brain wanted to worry about what this mysterious scribe had in store for me, but I refused to indulge it. I was living on borrowed time as it was, no sense wasting precious minutes guessing at outcomes I couldn't predict. Besides, even if this mysterious scribe didn't buy my story, I still had a few trump cards up my sleeve.

#

Trouble arrived two hours later.

Icarus had returned from one of his scouting trips and was softly talking to Dare somewhere behind me when the vibration hit us. A low hum from the horizon, lost at first under the crunch of our feet on the gravel and the howls of the cold winds. Rabbit recognized the danger first. His small body stiffened and his head lifted to the sky, like an animal's scenting the air.

"Bats," he whispered.

That little word was like a match igniting under a bundle of dried kindling. One second everyone froze, the next we scattered like roaches. I wasn't so used to disappearing at a moment's notice, so it took me a few additional, very precious seconds to catch on to the fact they were all suddenly climbing trees. Icarus grabbed me by my shirt collar and pulled me toward the nearest trunk.

"Climb. Quickly!"

Something in his voice told me not to argue. The tree he pushed me toward had a trunk covered with thorns and tiny, sharp twigs. Scrapes and cuts welled along my inner arms and face, but

I ignored them in my urgency to scramble up into the canopy. Icarus's pants and soft curses reached me as he climbed beneath me. Finally, I reached a large branch well-camouflaged by leaves. Icarus took a large branch a level below mine. "Hang on and try not to move."

Not a problem, I thought, looking down. From that height, a fall would result in multiple broken bones or possibly death. And that would be before the bats got a hold of your flesh.

The black cloud broke the horizon and the sun flashed off thousands of leathery black wings. Closer now, the hum turned into a high-pitched whirr. The vibrations shook me so hard my teeth rattled. I placed my hands over my ears to help muffle the sounds, but it didn't help much.

Bats were essentially robotic drones that patrolled the Bad Lands. If they detected any movement or noises indicating life, they would corner the potential prey and report back to the closest Troika substation, which would send out vampires after dark to investigate any anomalies.

All we had to do was stay still and quiet and the swarm would fly right past us. At least that was the ideal scenario.

But just before the black mass reached us, a loud crack sounded nearby. I lifted my head up and searched for the source. Time slowed. Not fifteen seconds later, a louder second crack exploded. A split second later, a child's shout. One second Rabbit had been clinging to his own branch in a tree several yards from the one Icarus and I perched on. The next, gravity pulled the kid toward the earth. He crashed through three smaller branches on his way down before finally grabbing onto one about ten feet from the ground.

"Shit," I whispered. Relief that he hadn't hit the ground was short-lived as the realization he was way too exposed sunk in. "We have to help him." I glanced over and saw Icarus scanning the area, like he was looking for solutions that weren't materializing. The hand I could see was reaching back as if to remove something from his pocket.

"Don't. Move." I didn't actually hear the words come from his mouth. It was more a combination of lip reading and my own mind telling me the same message. My mind and Icarus had nothing to worry about because I was frozen in fear. Over the years, I'd seen Troika officers laughing over footage of bats ripping apart animals. I knew they were designed to inflict ultimate pain and a slow, torturous death.

But before Icarus could do whatever he had planned, Dare decided he had taken too long to act. She leapt down from her own branch. Just when it looked like she was going to land on the same branch as Rabbit, her hand slipped. She plummeted toward the ground and landed in a heap. In the next moment, the swarm of bats reached the tree.

My heart tried to claw its way out of my chest.

I moved to leap down, but Icarus's shout stopped me.

"Do you want to die, too?"

"Of course not, but I can't just sit here and watch them get killed." I couldn't keep the accusation out of my voice. The judgment over his own assumed lack of interest in saving his team. Before he could answer or defend himself I started crawling out of my perch.

"Damn it!"

The high-pitched noises made my eardrums feel like they would burst any second. The thorns and branches bit into my hands. And behind me, Icarus launched creative curses after my retreating form. I focused on trying to reach Dare before the bats decided to attack. By the time my feet touched the ground, the kid was screaming for help. I didn't pause to see if Icarus followed me. I just launched myself toward Dare's too-still body.

The bats were circling the tree. I had to duck and roll to avoid the wide ribbon of claws and metal fangs.

"Six!" Rabbit called. "Help her!"

I nodded curtly, not making eye contact in case he'd see my fear. A few more running steps and I slid onto my side to land next to Dare. I curled my body around her, ducking my head over her shoulder to look into her face. Her eyes were closed and a nasty red wound pulsed on her scalp. A blood-smeared rock nearby told me she'd had the roughest possible landing.

The wings circling us kicked up a cyclone of wind. Small rocks, dry grass stalks and dirt got into my eyes, my mouth. I shied away from the stinging projectiles, but Dare didn't move. I wedged two fingers against her neck. The quadruple beat of her six-chambered vampire heart was dull but blessedly present.

Alive—for now.

I glanced over my shoulder to see Icarus climbing Rabbit's tree. Squinting, I cursed the coward for not helping me. Even if Dare regained consciousness and could fight, the two of us versus a swarm of blood-thirsty bats was no contest.

Why were they sitting there for so long? Were they toying with us? I felt my own thumping heartbeat and decided they were toying with us. Blood was best served warm, after all, and nothing warmed a human's blood like fear.

My eyes were scanning the immediate area for a weapon when the air shifted. Hard to tell what exactly. A lessening, I guess. I licked at my dry lips and tried to keep my legs from twitching despite the overwhelming urge to run. I curled tighter around Dare's body, hoping the position would afford us both some protection. And then, from what seemed a far distance, the sound of a concussion—almost like a bottle rocket—cut through the other noise, muted but distinctive. The noise sounded, the thump-thump-thump of my heart in my ears, the maddening flap of thousands of wings. And, finally, the entire swarm of bats took off like tiny bullets through the blue sky.

I didn't move for a long time. I'm not sure for how long, but it was well after the vibrations had quieted and the wind had died down and the sudden silence pressed in from all sides. Eventually, the undergrowth rustled and the sounds of breathing reached me. Jerking around from surprise, I turned to see Icarus's solemn face peering down at me.

He didn't offer a comforting touch of the arm or a polite inquiry about my well-being. Instead, he simply said, "Time to move."

"Wh—why did they leave so quickly?"

He held up a small device. I recognized it as the item I'd seen him pull from his pocket earlier. "Sonic charge."

He knelt down beside me and checked Dare's vitals. Using a dirty hand, he slapped at her cheeks and poured a little of our precious water supply on her lips. Eventually, she sputtered and came to cursing.

"What the fuck happened?" she demanded.

Icarus smiled down at her. It was the first time I'd seen the expression on his face and was shocked to find it utterly transformed his looks. The scars were less noticeable and it was hard not to think this Icarus was maybe a little likable. But then I remembered how he'd hung back while Dare lay so vulnerable on the ground. "You tried to be a hero," he said. "And almost got yourself killed." His expression didn't change despite the reprimand inherent in his words.

She gasped and tried to sit up. "The kid?"

Icarus and I pressed her back. Behind us, Rabbit called out. "I'm okay."

I turned to see Rabbit looking incredibly young and vulnerable as he leaned against a tree trunk like he needed its support. He forced a brave smile, but his hands were digging into the bark behind him. Then Icarus made some joke I didn't get—some sort of insider secret joke I wasn't invited to share. Rabbit laughed and Dare chuckled between wheezes.

While they talked, I checked over her limbs for broken bones. She gasped when I touched her ribs on the side she'd landed on, but I quickly realized they were bruised, not broken. Icarus met my gaze over her and raised a brow. "She'll live," I said. "But I'm worried about moving her."

He grimaced. "No choice. That diversion won't keep the bats away long. We need to double time to Book Mountain before dark."

We both glanced down at Dare, who'd been listening to the exchange. She licked her lips. "I'll be okay, I think. Just help me up,"

Together, we hefted her off the ground, ignoring the groans and hisses she couldn't keep in. Finally, after a little bit of wobbling, she managed to stand on her own. She had a goose egg on her forehead, a few bruised ribs and probably some nasty contusions down the right side of her body. I grabbed all her gear despite her protests while Rabbit found a long branch for her to lean on. When he ran back, holding it out to her like a trophy, she threw it aside. Ignoring the kid's hurt look, she raised her chin. "I can do this on my own."

With that she limped off with Rabbit trailing her with a hangdog expression. I stayed behind for a few moments. Tilting my head back, I look up at the perfectly blue sky with fat cotton wool clouds. If I squinted just right, the image totally filled my vision. For those few seconds, I could imagine I wasn't standing in the middle of a ravaged wasteland filled with vampires who wanted me dead—or worse. I could pretend that I was still young. Still five years old, laying in a field next to my mom, who pointed out clouds with interesting shapes. My eyes stung for those long ago days, back before the vampires came and mama died. I mourned for that little girl who had yet to suffer the touch of cold, dead hands.

"Six!" Dare yelled. "Move!"

# FIVE.

Three hours later, the sun was a bloody highlight along the horizon. Overhead the happy blue sky had dissolved into the inky twilight shadows. I smelled our destination before I saw it. The closer we got, the more the putrid cloud of rot and decay coated the nose and mouth. I covered my face with my elbow. "Christ, what is that smell?" I demanded through the crook of my elbow.

By this point, we'd come over a rise and could see the source of the stench. Spread out before us were dozens of mounds of garbage that seemed to stretch for miles. A large fence surrounded the place, but it was pocked with holes and fallen sections, like the people who created the landfill had even given up on it.

Icarus motioned ahead in a wide, sweeping gesture. "Welcome to the Book Mountain."

"Book Mountain?" I said. "More like Trash Mountain."

Icarus's eyebrows twitched with annoyance. "Under all that trash is one man's greatest treasure."

"Saga?" I said, repeating the name they'd mentioned.

"Only rebels get to call him by that name," Dare said. "You will call him 'The Scribe.'"

"Do you even know what a book is?" Icarus said, his tone insulting.

I frowned at him. "Of course." Although I hadn't seen an actual book in years, I still hadn't forgotten how precious they were to my mother. Our little apartment was filled with rickety bookcases made from cinder blocks and wood. Mom used to leave paperbacks all over the house so she'd never be more than an arm's length away from one of her precious books.

The rusted metal gates were covered in pits and flakes of paint. A drunken sign hanging from the top warned trespassers to keep out.

I rolled my eyes. "That gate wouldn't keep an infant out."

A smile lifted the corner of Icarus's mouth. "Don't let it fool you. Saga has plenty of booby traps throughout this place. Keep your eyes open and be ready to duck and roll."

The gate screeched a warning but offered no other resistance. Beyond it, as far as I could see, were mountains of trash. Rusted out cadavers of automobiles, wheel-less baby carriages, old clothes waving in the breeze like flags of surrender. Hills made of plastic bottles and used diapers. Aluminum cans, cereal boxes, containers made of something Icarus called Styrofoam. After years spent in the sterile halls of the dormitories and the crisp, modern palaces of the Troika's leaders, this pit of rot and decay was a shock to the system. A morbid museum documenting the consumption habits of pre-war humans.

As we passed a tall pile of shoes, Icarus stopped and started digging. I looked down at my feet. By that time, the shoes the Chatelaine had given me were meager scraps that barely covered my feet. The places where they'd worn away were covered in weeping blisters and cuts from two days of walking. Still, I hesitated to dive in like Dare and Rabbit did the instant Icarus gave the nod. Rabbit emerged from the pile with a victorious whoop. He had a boot in each hand. The set didn't match—one was black, the other brown—but they appeared to be the same size. Without hesitation, he kicked off his threadbare sandals.

"Damn," the kid said. "Too big." He glanced around. Seeing that Dare was in the process of putting on some she'd found, his gaze shot to me. "Here." He thrust the prizes toward me. I hesitated. The kid frowned at me. "What's wrong?"

"Miss Priss probably thinks her tender feet are

too good for second-hand shoes." This came from Dare. Hers matched, but that's about as much as they had going for them.

I avoided her too-knowing glare and grabbed the boots from Rabbit. "Thanks, kid."

They were still warm and gritty from his feet. I ignored my natural urge to recoil and shoved my foot in all the way. It was only when the leather cupped my heel that I realized the damned things fit like they'd been made for my foot.

"Ha! Look at that," Rabbit said, beaming.

I glanced down at our feet. Mine with the mismatched but well-made boots and Rabbits bare and covered in dirt and blood. Shame washed through me. This kid had never in his life known the luxury of new shoes. I smiled at him. "Let's find you some now."

"Here, buddy," Icarus called from across the pile. He tossed a pair of scuffed wingtips across. The kid looked like he'd been handed gold. "Wow, thanks Ick!"

I raised my brows at the nickname and received a grimace in return. "Put them on quick. Saga's waiting."

#

A couple of minutes later, Icarus led us to a pile of old cars. I glanced around, expecting a pack of junkyard dogs or a swarm of bats to attack at any moment. Even among the mountains of trash, we were way too exposed for my liking.

Ignoring my worried glances, Icarus took his time finding a stone from the red dirt. Once he found a specimen he liked he sucked at his teeth while he squinted at the pile. A split second before I opened my mouth to ask what he was doing, he threw the rock at the rusted hood of a blue car about halfway up the pile.

Just when I was ready to call bullshit, a small mechanical sound reached my ear. Like small gears grinding. An instant later a headlight from a red car lower on the stack broke away from the car's frame. It rose up on a telescoping rod and once it reached about twelve inches up, the top portion flipped over to reveal a camera's eye imbedded inside.

I raised my brows and shot Dare a look. She shot back a shit-eating grin. Then she mugged for the camera and gave it a wave. Icarus just stood with his legs braced and his jaw tight, which from what I could tell was his relaxed stance.

A red light blinked to the right of the eye, but no voices came from the cars and no armies appeared from the surrounding trash piles. Instead, another mechanical sound followed by a whoosh of air escaping some sort of airlock sent a puff of rusty dust up from the trunk of a large sedan.

Icarus motioned a hand toward the yawning trunk. "After you."

I considered suggesting he go fuck himself, but paused. We'd come to this place so I could be tested. Something told me to balk at going in first would earn me a failing grade before I'd even crossed the threshold. So instead of arguing, I raised my chin, adjusted my canteen on its shoulder strap and took a purposeful step toward the dark void.

"Watch your step," Rabbit warned. "That first one's tricky." The helpful suggestion earned the kid a knock on the shoulder from Dare. He shot her an annoyed look as he massaged the tender spot. "What? We don't want her to die before Saga gets his hands on her."

The way he said it implied that surviving to meet Saga might be worse than death, but I ignored it, shot him a nod of thanks for the warning and marched forward.

My new heavy boots clomped against the metal bumper. The instant my feet hit the inside of the trunk, the bottom gave way and blue shadows swallowed me down a long, cold throat. Gravity tugged me down even as my stomach shot up to the back of my throat, blocking the screams that fought for freedom. My back hit something hard and then my side did too. I was in some sort of chute. I couldn't see anything and the air was clogged with dust and the cold, grey scent of clay. I could only brace myself, hoping that whatever waited for me at the bottom wasn't instantly lethal.

Soon enough, the world slowed down and then went still altogether. Before I opened my eyes, I did a quick physical inventory. When the pains in my arms, legs and back proved to be superficial, I listened for a moment. I could hear sounds, like arguing, echoing far above my head. The others were trying to decide who'd come in after me. But closer, down there where I lay on my side in the dark, I heard something far more menacing—the sound of an animal breathing.

"Be very still," a male voice said from maybe twenty feet away—hard to tell since the words echoed off the walls like we were inside some sort of cavern. "Polonius hasn't had his rations yet this day."

I opened my eyes and was pleased to find they'd adjusted to the dark enough to allow me to make out the outline of a bent-male form standing next to a very large four-legged animal. "Maybe Polonius should be careful, too," I said. "I haven't had any rations today, either."

A low chuckle reached me. "You hide your fear. That's good. But is it enough? We shall see."

I pushed myself out of my prone position to turn toward the voice. "Show yourself, old man."

A light flared. Pain burst behind my pupils at the sudden brightness. I covered them for a moment and then squinted toward the man. I had to blink a few times before the blurry form took shape, but when it did, I dropped my hand and let my lids open wide.

Standing next to the largest dog I had ever seen was the oldest man I had ever seen.

Granted, in the post-Troika world, men rarely lived longer than their thirtieth birthday. Even those who'd been blessed (or cursed depending on your perspective) with a desirable blood type, still aged rapidly because of the constant demands on their veins. And those who worked in the blood camps literally were worked to an early grave.

But the man before me had to be at least double that, but I didn't really have much to judge by. His shoulders slumped forward, as if he was curling into himself. He had a long, white beard, which he'd braided into a long, thick strand. In contrast to the hair on his face, his scalp was completely free of hair and the dome shone dully in the lantern light. His clothes were simple grey homespun—clean from what I could see and functional but completely free of ornamentation. In his right hand, he held a lantern aloft and in his left was a wood staff taller than his own height. The wood was highly polished and topped with a metal symbol I couldn't make out from where I stood.

"Now that you've had your look," he said, "and I've had mine, you can tell me your name, stranger."

I licked my dry lips. "My birth name is Carmina Sargosa." I'd chosen to give him that name first because he seemed old enough to know the history of my mother.

His eyes widened. "Sargosa, you say? Hmm.

And what name did they give you at the camp?"

"I don't come from the camps."

He pursed his lips. "Don't try to convince me you grew up in the resistance. You've got too many teeth in that mouth of yours."

My lips quirked. "I was raised in the Dormitories."

He stilled. "Which one?"

"Meridian."

"Let me guess—cell six?"

I nodded. He'd known who I was all along. Those questions had been a test of my honesty.

He cocked his head. "What a coincidence. Someone named Meridian Six is wanted for attacking the Prime just two nights past."

I crossed my arms. "Shouldn't believe rumors." For that matter how in the hell did he hear anything hiding as he did down in that pit.

Swishing sounds came from behind me, indicating the others were on their way down the chute to join us. Icarus appeared first, of course. Unlike me, he didn't flail out of the tube and land on his ass. Instead he found his feet easily and came to join the old man and me. "What's the story?" he asked Saga.

He flicked too-shred eyes in my direction. "I'm intrigued. Bring her." With that he turned flicking a, "Come Polonius" over his shoulder.

The dog executed a wide turn and followed his slow master back through the archway leading out of the cavern. I looked at Icarus. "What now?"

Rabbit and Dare shot out of the slide a split second before he said, "Now we find out if you get to live."

#

As it turned out, the cavern I'd landed in was only a tiny part of what turned out to be an extensive underground bunker. Icarus and the others led me into a long corridor. The walls of this space were covered floor to ten-foot ceiling with books. The musty scent of aged pages filled the space, and I wondered how Saga managed to keep the books from rotting in the damp air. Icarus moved ahead to go talk to Saga, leaving me in Dare's keeping.

"What is this place?" I asked her. Because of her wounds, I had to slow my pace, which was fine given the judgment waiting for me at the other end of corridor.

She glanced at me but I could tell she wasn't happy to have to talk. "Saga considers himself a historian, of sorts. This is his library."

I glanced at the thousands of books. "What kind of historian?"

"Of the human race."

My eyes widened. I knew that when the Troika decided to take over the planet, one of their first moves was buying up all media companies, which included servers filled with the bulk of shared knowledge on the planet. When the actual war began, it was simply a matter of flipping a few switches to deprive humans of every electronic source of communication and information.

"Where did he get all these? I thought the Troika confiscated all the remaining printed books when they took over."

"They did. But Saga went underground long before the war began."

"What? Why would he do that?"

She sniffed, like my curiosity offended her. But before she could explain, Saga's voice echoed down the hall. "Because I never trusted the world wide web. Too many spiders."

My instinct was to declare the old man insane. But I knew all too well how easily the Troika had cut people off from each other because they'd sacrificed their freedoms to the gods of convenience.

Dare nudged me toward the doorway that Saga's voice had come from. I stumbled across the portal and gasped. I thought the hallway had a lot of books, but the—well 'room' was too pitiful a word—I'd just entered had more books than I ever imagined existed. The room was really a wide, round circle that rose dozens of feet in the air. Like a silo of books. Tall, rickety ladders leaned against the towering shelves and walkways were built at intervals up the walls. In the center of the room, a large desk stood atop a platform reached by a narrow bridge. Other bridges wagon-wheeled out at intervals to the shelves. The tunnel of books continued far below, as well, and those appeared to be accessed by ladders leading down from the bridges.

"Tell me, Carmina, can you read?"

I considered telling him to call me Six, but the twinkle in his eye told me he'd used my real name on purpose. "Of course." It wouldn't do for the Troika's propaganda doll to be ignorant.

"What is your favorite book?"

When a man who owns more books than the number of humans left on the planet asks you your favorite book it's not a casual question. This was the beginning of the tests. I raised my chin and went with the truth. "I've never read a printed book, and the majority of story-discs I was allowed to read were written by vampires loyal to the Troika."

"No doubt they were heroic tales about brave vampires who defeated hordes of dirty humans."

My lips twitched. "You've read *Blood Bond*, then?"

"Among others." He clicked his tongue. "Pedestrian writing, at best. At worst, they're terrifying windows into the psyche of our masters."

"What's your favorite book?" I asked him. Not that I knew the titles of many human novels, but I figured a man like Saga would jump at the chance to talk about his favorite stories. Maybe he'd appreciate it so much he'd go lighter on me in the trials.

"*Fahrenheit 451*," he said immediately. "You've

heard of it."

I nodded. "Bradbury."

His eyes flared. "I'm impressed."

"Don't be. The only reason I know of it was one of my teachers preached it as the perfect example of how humans were begging to be dominated by a superior species."

"Oh." Saga's face fell. So did my hopes of passing his tests.

Behind me Rabbit cleared his throat. "My favorite is *Watership Down*."

I frowned at him. "You can read?"

"Of course." Rabbit puffed up his chest. "I ain't a dumbass."

I smiled at the kid in apology. "What's that one about?" I wanted to keep the kid talking in hopes it would help Saga forget I'd insulted his favorite book.

"*Watership Down* is about a group of heroic rabbits who have to leave their warren in order to find a new home."

"That's why he's called Rabbit," Dare offered with an indulgent smile at the kid.

I nodded politely, wondering how anyone could sound so loyal to a silly story about rabbits. "That's nice," I said when they all looked at me expectantly.

Saga's eyes narrowed. "What do you remember of your mother?"

The question was so sudden, so unexpected that hearing it felt like a physical blow. A sucker punch. Surely he knew. "That she was the leader of the human resistance at the Battle of Manhattan."

He pursed his lips and ran a hand down his beard. "Do you believe this information to be true?"

I raised my chin. "Doesn't matter what I believe. I know it to be true because I remember her."

"Are you certain?"

"Of course."

He smiled sadly, like one might at a misguided child. "Are you aware that the Troika has been doing experiments on humans for years in the work camps?"

I crossed my arms. "I've heard whispers, rumors."

Icarus snorted. "They're not just rumors." He sounded too confident for the information to be from hearsay.

I shrugged because I didn't have a response. They'd tell me what they wanted me to know soon enough.

Saga saw me mentally dig my heels in and smiled. "Isn't it possible they also conducted experiments on the humans they collected for the dormitories?"

I narrowed my eyes and tilted my head. "The Troika is capable of a lot of things, but they are not able to falsify memories or emotions. And if you know what is good for you, you will stop trying to convince me that the memories I have of my mother are lies." I delivered these words in a voice edged with steel. It simply was not an option to even entertain what they were suggesting. My memories of my mother were the only warmth I had to cling to when I was young and huddled in the cold, white dormitory bed at night. When it was dark and the sniffling of my cellmates punctuated the air and the loneliness pressed in so hard I could barely breath. The fact Saga even attempted to fuck with my head like this made me want to walk out of that book tomb and damn the consequences.

"I wouldn't act on the thoughts behind those wild eyes of yours."

"You don't know what I think, old man."

He dipped his chin to acknowledge that he didn't have the ability to mind read. "I wouldn't presume to, but I can see the anger boiling there. But it is displaced. We aren't your enemies."

"Aren't you? Ever since the Chatelaine brought me to this group I have been treated like one."

"Do you know what the human rebels call you?" Saga asked. I shook my head. "The Troika's Concubine."

"Why dress it up in big words, Scribe? You meant to say I was the Troika's whore, correct?" I asked with a raised brow.

"I still say we shouldn't trust someone whose reputation is pro-Troika." Dare grumbled.

I couldn't afford for these people to see how

their obtuseness over the reality of my life with the Troika affected me, so I tossed my hair back and raised my chin. "So why didn't you kill me on sight?"

"For some reason the Chatelaine trusted you. That saved you at first." Icarus met my eyes. "You will only remain alive if you can prove yourself useful to the cause."

I'd had enough. I was tired of being told what I would or would not do. I crossed my arms and looked him in the eye. "You can shove your cause up your ass. I don't answer to you."

Hard metal slammed into my soft temple. Ripples of pain pulsed through my head, but fear was strangely absent. Shock, probably. Or just resignation. It wasn't the first time a man had pressed a gun to my head. Castor loved a little gun play before he fucked my vein. More times than I could count, I'd taunt him into rages hoping he'd just pull the trigger.

But Icarus wasn't Castor and I hadn't escaped only to die less than forty-eight hours later. I gritted my teeth against the pain and glared into his eyes. "Fine, you want information?" I'd give them something they couldn't refuse. Then they'd have to let me go. "I can tell you how to destroy the Troika."

Dare snorted. "Bullshit."

The gun's pressure didn't ease up, but Icarus's eyes narrowed. "Explain."

I licked my dry lips. Time to talk fast. "Rebels

have been fighting minor skirmishes with the Troika for years, but not making any major headway, right?" He nodded reluctantly. "Well, what if you could deal a major blow to the vamps' infrastructure?"

"I'm listening."

"Do you know who Pontius Morordes is?"

"He's a murderer," Icarus spat.

I glanced at him but the hatred in his eyes made me look away quickly. Good thing then that I didn't mention that I knew Morordes by more than just name. He'd attended several of the Troika parties where I'd been paraded out like a show pony. Unlike the other vampires who pawed me and looked me over like an *objet d'art*, he'd had a kindly smile and seemed to look down on the others who treated humans like toys. I'd even visited him at his lab a few times. Sure, he'd taken my blood and done a few tests, but he'd always had a ready smile and a gentle manner. Still, I didn't object to Icarus's characterization because I figured it wouldn't be very good for my health.

"In the camps they call him Doctor Death," Icarus said. "For years he's been collecting human specimens and conducting experiments. Many of which have left the test subjects mutilated or dead. What of him?"

I stretched my neck a little, trying to get some room between me and the bullet-spitter, but it followed me. "A few months ago he figured out a prototype for synthetic blood."

The Scribe and Icarus exchanged a dubious look. "Synthetic?"

I nodded. "They've been having trouble in the blood camps. The stress of constant bleeding is killing off a lot of the humans, and the breeding program isn't producing enough people to replace them fast enough." Because blood type is determined by genetics, the Troika had to have enough humans of the right blood types to procreate a new generation of sacrificial lambs. Since children couldn't survive long in the bloodletting wards, the Troika had logistical problems. Along the way, one of their scientists proposed the idea of creating a synthetic alternative to human blood as insurance against a blood shortage.

"The Troika would never give up High Bloods," Saga said. High Blood was the name for humans with the most desirable blood types. Like me.

I swallowed as I quickly decided how much to share, which was as little as possible. "Before I escaped, I overheard that they were starting a program to try to breed more AB types."

"The camps are filled with mostly Os," Icarus said. "If they're trying to make more ABs, they'll keep those offspring for the Troika's officials and give the synthetic blood to the lower level vampires."

Instead of blood type, vampires were judged

based on the purity of their genetic line. The Troika's officials all came from the most pure vampire lines, while the rest of the vampire population came from lineages soiled by human blood.

"So the synthetic is for the plebs? Why make it at all?"

I nodded. "I heard Castor talking to his cabinet about some riots in the city over blood rationing. They're hoping the synthetic blood will mollify the plebeian vamps."

The Scribe scrubbed his hand over his face. "Which means they won't need the blood camps anymore."

"Right. The officials will still have their stables of High Bloods and the Troika will always need labor camps, but the humans in the blood camps will become ... obsolete."

"Shit," Dare breathed.

"It gets worse," I began. Now that I was knee-deep in this story, I realized how horrible the news I brought them actually was. It was one thing for me to hear the Troika discussing their plans in the plush rooms of the compound. It was something else entirely to share the information with humans who for all I knew might have relatives or friends in those camps. But considering one of the people I was telling the story to had a gun pointed at my head, I was pretty sure I couldn't just change my mind. "Once they had a synthetic blood, they had another problem to solve. Humans are dying rapidly in the camps, but there are still millions of people hooked up to bleeding machines that will be obsolete once they roll out the blood."

Dare cursed under her breath. The Scribe went white. And the mouth of Icarus's gun bit harder into my skin. Grimacing, I soldiered on. "That's when Castor had what he's calling his most brilliant plan to date. He called it 'The Factory.'"

As soon as the words left my mouth, the room fell dead silent. Even Polonius had frozen, like he sensed danger on the air.

"Where is it?" Icarus asked, his tone grave.

The Scribe twitched like he'd just been zapped by a thought. "So that's what it is," he breathed, almost to himself.

"What do you mean?" Dare demanded of the old man.

He shuffled away, his lips moving as he muttered to himself. "It's here somewhere." With gnarled hands, he began shuffling through stacks of paper on the large table. Icarus looked at Dare and she shrugged. Since he had the gun on me, she went to investigate.

"What are you looking for, Saga?" she asked in a patient, kind tone that told me she was well-used to the old man wandering off and speaking to people who weren't there.

"It was here." More shuffling. "I didn't know what it was. But then she— Yes, hmm. Perhaps over here." He moved to the other end of the table and started going through another sheaf of papers. Whatever he was looking for, it was clear our conversation wouldn't continue until he'd completed his search. Awkward for me, considering the gun.

"Is the gun still necessary?" I asked conversationally.

Icarus's lips tightened into a frown. "Quiet."

Before I could react to that, The Scribe bellowed, "Aha! I knew it was here."

"What is it?" Dare asked, moving closer to inspect the paper in his hand.

"A few weeks ago, one of the patrols in sector four reported some building activity near the river. They brought me that drawing."

Dare frowned at the sheet as she walked over to share it with Icarus. I craned my neck to catch a glimpse, but before I could see more than what looked like a building with three chimneys, she jerked it away. "Well, it certainly looks like a factory," Dare offered.

"When Jeremiah brought it to me, I dismissed it," The Scribe said, "but when the girl told us about it I remembered a detail I'd found odd at the time." He pointed a hand to the paper. The land around the building was covered in a spider's web of parallel lines.

"Train tracks, probably," Icarus said. "So?"

"So the Troika have transportation rovers to handle large shipments of goods," Saga said. "Why suddenly use trains?"

I knew the answer, but I kept silent. Better to let them figure it out than to be blamed for the truth once it hit them.

"They'll have to make large batches of synthetic blood. Maybe trains can carry more—"

The Scribe shook his head. "That factory isn't producing synthetic blood."

Icarus frowned. "What do you mean? She said they built the factory to make synthetic blood."

"No, I didn't," I said in a small voice.

"Then what are they making there?" Dare asked.

I swallowed hard and looked at The Scribe, who I could see was already well ahead of the others. "They're not making anything there but ashes."

Icarus lowered the gun and his face morphed into a mask of denial. "They ... no." He paused, shook himself. "No!" He kicked a pile of books taller than his head. The colorful spines came crashing down with what remained of his illusions.

Saga remained silent and grim-faced, despite the abuse Icarus was dealing to his precious books. Dare made a distressed sound and hurried to soothe him. I turned my back on both of them and went to join Saga. "Can you show me where this is on a map?" I said quietly.

The old man hesitated, but finally nodded and walked over to the desk. Behind me, Dare spoke softly to Icarus. His anger filled the room like smoke. Saga slowly unrolled a large map across the surface. He used small stacks of books to anchor each of the four corners. I squinted at the hand-drawn image of the area that used to be called New York City.

Almost immediately following the war, the Troika government had redrawn borders to turn the United States into three distinct regions, each controlled by one of The Prime's handpicked governors. But the center of power for the Troika remained in New York, since it was during that final battle that they crippled the human forces enough to finally surrender the entire war. They'd renamed the city Nachtstadt—Night City—and destroyed every human landmark in the center of the city and replaced them with vampire-designed towers and monuments to the Prime.

The map showed not just Nachtstadt, which now included parts of old New Jersey—over the river where Hoboken used to be. My brain flashed up a painful image of the old Victorian mom and I used to live in that overlooked the Lincoln Tunnel. It had drafty windows and creaky floors, but its walls had been filled with mostly happy memories.

See? I said to myself, they're wrong. Those are my memories. My very real memories.

I looked up from the map at Saga. "You drew this?"

He nodded. "Brooklyn born and raised." His pride was evident both by his tone and the way he lovingly depicted the outskirts of the city, where the structures built by humans still slouched like crumbling *memento mori*.

Saga tapped a calloused finger near the top of the map, near the river. "According to the patrol, the building is about here."

I nodded and studied the map. "What is the date?"

He frowned. "Why?"

"Because when I last heard about the Factory, the impression I got was construction was almost done. I'm trying to figure out how long you have until they fire up those furnaces."

He told me the date. I looked up quickly. "Almost time for the Blood Moon."

Saga looked equally impressed and worried. "They'd want to baptize their new project in the light of their most sacred moon."

"Three nights isn't much time for you to make a plan."

He tilted his head toward me. "Why do you keep saying 'you' instead of 'we,' child?"

I stood up straighter. "What do you mean? You wanted information. I gave it to you. I'm free to go now?"

A bitter laugh echoed through the cavernous room. "You're not really that naive, are you?"

I turned to face Icarus with my hands on my hips. But before I could respond, Dare pointed an accusing finger at me. "She's lying! They sent her here to trap us!"

It took about every ounce of strength in my body not to roll my eyes at her. "Your own people confirmed that the factory exists."

"They confirmed something looking like a factory is being built." She crossed her arms. "And even if it's really what you say it's for, we could still show up and find an army of vampires waiting to kill us."

I laughed. "If you think the Troika sees your pathetic little team as enough of a threat to orchestrate an elaborate scheme like staging my escape, you're not just misguided—you're delusional. The Chatelaine brought me to you, remember? I didn't seek you out. None of this has anything to do with me. I just want to move on and try to cobble a life together."

They stared at me like I'd spoken in a foreign language. "It has everything to do with you," Saga said. "And if you think we want anything different than that life you just spoke of, you're the one who's delusional. Do you think we enjoy living underground and running from bat patrols? Like it or not, you're just as involved in all this as we are now. More, maybe."

I didn't like where this was going. "Look, I didn't escape the Troika only to get involved in some scheme that would put me back into their crosshairs. I'm sorry if people are going to die, but I don't plan on being one of them."

The unmistakable sound of a gun cocking made my heart skip a beat. I turned slowly. Dare had taken Icarus's ancient six-shooter and pointed it at my head. I was getting tired of people pointing weapons at me, but she looked determined enough for this not to be an idle threat. "You don't get to pretend to have a choice in this." Her hand shook a little, but I didn't mistake it for fear. Anger drove Dare. "Your days of sitting in the ivory tower are over sweetheart. It's time to get your hands dirty."

She had no idea how dirty my hands were, and I wanted to punch her for believing my life had been anything close to easy. But I didn't want that gun to start shouting. "Whoa," I said, "let's not get emotional here."

She blinked. "Not get emotional?" she snorted. "I lost the luxury of emotion the day they took my family."

I frowned at her. "But you're a vampire—"

She laughed like rusty nails scoring metal. "Not all vampires hate humans. Some of us loved them."

"So when you say your family, you mean ... "

Her hand tightened on her gun. "My husband and daughter."

I cursed quietly. "I'm sorry."

"No you're not!" she barked suddenly. Cold fear rose up my spine. Before she'd been angry, but now she looked crazy and fully capable of murder. "While you were sucking the Troika's cocks, my daughter was murdered and hung to bleed out from the window of our apartment building to serve as a warning to the other vampires who were considering mating with humans."

"Dare," Icarus said, his voice quiet, "put down the gun."

Her jaw clenched and she looked entirely capable of ignoring his demand. Her fingers white-knuckled on the stock and her index finger twitched toward the trigger. Cold sweat beaded on my forehead and my eyes scanned the area for weapons and escape routes. The latter wasn't an option given we were on a platform suspended above a cavern of books. Even if I could jump down without breaking my leg, I'd be like a fish in a barrel.

"Look, I'm not your enemy and this isn't my war," I said in what I hoped was a reasonable tone. "I'm leaving at sunrise."

Dare's gun flashed menacingly in the light. "My friend Colt here says otherwise."

It only took a few moments to make my decision. Dare talked a good game, but I didn't really believe she'd kill me. All the resistance members in the world couldn't compete with the insider's knowledge I had of the Troika's top tier officials. I was worth way more alive to them than dead. Of the three, only Dare posed a real physical threat, even injured as she was.

I relaxed my shoulders and expression into what I hoped was a mask of defeat. Dare's eyes narrowed, but her grip on the gun relaxed a fraction. The instant I saw her buy my ruse, I ducked my shoulder and crashed into her midsection. As in slow motion I pivoted off her stomach and twisted, launching off my back foot into a dead run. Behind me, I heard a shouted curse and a worried exclamation from the old man. I didn't slow when a crash sounded, and I sure as hell didn't stick around to find out if Dare's friend had anything to say.

I leapt off the end of the catwalk and ducked into the tunnel. Once the musty scent of the cramped space hit my nose, I realized my error. I'd entered the underground bunker through a slide. Hardly an ideal exit route. But I didn't have the extra seconds to spare scrambling around for an alternate exit. I skidded into the cavern where I'd first met Saga and scrambled when my foot caught on a rock sticking up from the packed earth. I was three steps from the chute leading toward freedom when a heavy weight slammed into my back like a wrecking ball. I fell face-first into the cold, packed dirt and every molecule of air in my body escaped in a painful rush. A low, mean growl hit my ear like a hot wind.

"Good boy, Polonius." Saga's voice sounded amused but winded. "Miss Six, that canine on your back is trained to attack on my word. Are you going to force me to utter that word or are you going to be a good girl and surrender."

Warm drool landed on my neck. Polonius was hungry. My own stomach growled in response.

As much as I wanted to stand up and fight, I knew that even if I managed to get away from the dog and up that chute before Saga gave the command, I'd never make it out in the Badlands with no food, water or provisions. So, as much as it pained, me I lowered my forehead to the red earth and surrendered.

# SIX.

The cell was darker than the Badlands during a new moon. My hand was on a cold stone wall, but the dirt floors made it smell like a grave. Tears stung the corners of my eyes. I swiped at them even though no one could see me. It was bad enough I had to be with myself and those fucking tears. They sickened me.

A specter of a memory haunted my brain. Of lying in a similar cell, only that old one was all-white and brighter than lightning. Back then I'd been crying too. But those tears had been innocent and pure. A child mourning the loss of everything familiar, a child's fear of the unknown. That was my first night in the dormitories. They'd taken me straight there after they'd realized my blood type. Back then, I didn't know how that simple test would determine my fate. I'd been so relieved they'd let me live that I hadn't thought about what a bleak existence it would become without my mother.

I remembered blood stains on my hands contrasting sharply against crisp, white sheets. A few tears mixed with the red like some morbid watercolor painting. I remembered feeling like I was being watched even though I was alone in the room. I remembered feeling like my heart was going to claw its way out of my chest and run away without me. I remembered feeling more alone than any other girl in the history of the world. But I'd learned quickly that tears only made the beatings worse, and the more I stuffed them down, the stronger I became.

But back then I'd had a future, even if I hadn't known it. Now? Even if they let me live until morning and forced me to help them attack the Troika, it was doubtful I'd last the week.

The sound of a key in a lock echoed. I swiped away the tears and sat up. They couldn't be allowed to see me broken. Even if—especially if—they planned to kill me.

Only instead of Icarus or Dare arriving with a gun, my visitor was Rabbit, bearing a tray of food. A lantern on the tray created a halo of light around his young face. "You hungry?" he whispered.

I nodded, but only because I didn't want him to leave. That kid was the closest thing I had to a friend in Book Mountain. Hell, he was the closest thing I had in the entire world.

He smirked and set the tray down on the floor next to the bed. "It ain't much. Saga says we can't spare too much since we might have to go underground again soon."

I accepted a small cup of water with a nod. "Go underground?"

"Yeah, Dare said we're going to make big move on the mosquitos, but after we might have to hide for a while."

I froze. "Wait, you said 'we're'—as in you're going to help with the attack?"

He nodded with exaggerated patience. "Of course. I'm really helpful." His tone was heavy with offense, like I'd wounded his pride. "Icarus said I'm going to be really important to this mission."

I shouldn't have been surprised Icarus was going to let the kid take part, but I was shocked Dare was allowing it. She watched over Rabbit like he was her own young. "Hey Rabbit?"

"Yeah?" he said over a mouthful of dried meat I'd refused when he offered it to me.

"Did they say what they're going to do with me?"

A shadow filled the doorway, blocking out the dim light from the hallway. I recognized Dare's petite silhouette. "Rabbit," she snapped, "Saga needs help in the library."

The kid flashed me an apologetic look. I smiled back and shoved the rest of the dried meat strips into his hand. That earned me a real smile before he ducked out of the room. Dare stood aside to let him pass. The tenderness with which she'd watched him fled the minute he exited. Then those eyes hardened and watched my reaction as she slowly closed us in together.

The meager light from the lantern didn't do much to expel the shadows standing between the vampire and me. Her yellow eyes glowed in the dark. She didn't approach immediately. Just stood with her back to the door, letting the tension rise between us like a poisonous gas. I might be damned but I wasn't going to be the first one to speak.

Finally, she pulled away from the wall. "Have you ever tasted blood?"

The question was so unexpected, I jerked in shock. With a wary frown, I hesitated. "Yes."

"Whose?"

I licked my dry lips. "My own."

She nodded and took her time absorbing this information. "By your own choice?"

I looked up and met her eyes. "No." I'd expected this information to please her. Instead she grimaced and looked away.

"We're not all monsters, you know." She looked back at me, to make sure I'd heard. I didn't react. Her posture was tense and her mood too unpredictable for me to want to give her any reaction that might set off a chain reaction. "I haven't had blood fresh from the source in years." She paused. When she spoke again her tone was quiet, like a confession. "And I've never had any high blood."

I stilled like an animal sensing impending attack. "Dare—"

She shook her head. "Don't worry. I'm not here to feed from you." She reached into her jacket and removed Icarus's old Colt. "I'm here for this."

Perhaps I should have felt shocked. Or scared. Or ... something. Instead, a weary numbness settled deep into my bones. Holding her gaze, I rose from the cot. She raised the gun a little higher in warning. I raised my hands out to the side and raised my chin. "Just be done with it."

Her eyes widened. "You're not going to ask me to spare you?"

I shook my head. "What's the point?"

"You're pathetic," she spat.

I lowered my arms. "What do you want from me? To beg for a life that never belonged to me in the first place? To fight for the chance to let another set of masters use me? I'm done being anyone's whore, Dare." I jerked my head toward the gun. "Do it."

The gun lowered a fraction. She stared at me intently for a full thirty seconds before she spoke. "What did they do to you?"

I squeezed my eyes together, but a traitorous tear escaped to roll down my cheek. "Just do it," I gritted out through clenched teeth.

"Six? Look at me."

I heaved out a harsh breath and opened my eyes, prepared to let her have it for dragging this out to the point of torture. But when I saw the look on her face, the numbness was burned off as hot anger roared to life. But before I could scream at her or rush her and punch the pity from her face, she spoke again. "You stink of them, you know. Their scent clings to you."

Now it was shame's turn to make an appearance. "Then you know what they did."

She tilted her head. "I thought the concubine thing was just an insult because you spoke on behalf of the Troika."

I laughed bitterly. "In exchange for my services to the Troika's propaganda machine, I was passed around like a trophy among the highest level vampires. It was something of a badge of honor to vein fuck Alexis Sargosa's daughter." Now that I was talking, the words spilled out like bile. "Some only kept me a few days. Others claimed me for months, a couple for years. Those ones delighted in turning me into their personal slave. I did everything from clean their silver to playing a starring role in their sadistic games. A few were kind compared to the others and educated me to amuse themselves. One or two preferred me to fight back so they taught me how to use weapons and my fists. Then they'd delight in disarming me and delivering punishment for being too good a student. But mostly I just served as a blood dispenser."

She'd lowered the gun and crossed her arms. "That's why you finally left. You couldn't stand it anymore?"

"No." Now that I'd admitted so much, I decided it wouldn't hurt to offer one last confession before I met the maker. "I left because after enduring their tortures, they found the one invasion I could not endure."

She frowned.

I laughed, but the sound felt flat to my own ears. "You haven't put it together yet?" I didn't wait for her to confirm what I already knew to be true. "Several months ago, the Prime came to me with good news. I was going to be given a great honor. The Troika officials loved my sweet blood so much that they were going to make me the first brood mare in their blood stables."

Dare gasped softly but I was beyond offering consolation.

"According to him, I was going to be put in a special dormitory and given my choice of men of high blood with whom to mate. If any of the children I created turned out to be AB-, they would be raised in the most favorable conditions and be given the honor of becoming concubines to the top Troika officials."

"And if they weren't high blooded?"

I looked her in the eye and ignored the phantom pain in my stomach. "Aborted."

The silence in the room was complete. Unlike

the last time, it wasn't a silent gulf that kept two foes separated. Instead, those quiet moments were filled with shared knowledge of duty and loss and the longing for a tiny heartbeat against the skin.

"The night I left?" My hand went to my belly. "They just had informed me that I was to be impregnated again. I couldn't go through that again—the loss." I looked up again and saw empathy in her yellow gaze. "But more than that, I was terrified it would work this time and they wouldn't abort it. How could I doom a child to my life?"

She watched me silently for a few moments. Tension zinged through the space between us like lightning. Finally, she sucked in a long, slow breath. "How can you say you want to run? They took your mother. They took your life." She stepped forward and pointed at my stomach. "They took your child. They took your choices away. How can you just run when you have every cause to turn around and fight back?"

I blinked to stall the tears. "Because I want a chance to live for whatever time I have left."

She snorted. "Running isn't the same as living."

"Unbelievable." I shook my head at her. "You walked in here ready to kill me, but now you're angry that I'm not trying hard enough to live."

She made a disgusted sound and shoved the gun into her rear waistband. "I wasn't going to kill you. He just told me to scare you a little until you agreed to help us."

I crossed my arms. "That's what I don't get. Why would you want the Troika's whore to help you?"

She licked her lips and glanced sideways. "Look I— I'm sorry about that. But see it from my perspective. You showed up all glowing and healthy and with your reputation preceding you. How could I not be suspicious of you?"

I laughed bitterly and lifted my shirt. Her eyes widened when she saw the patterns of bruises and scars covering my abdomen and torso. "They made sure the skin that showed was clean for the camera, but the rest was open season. And as for my reputation, well, I gave you credit for being too smart to believe their propaganda."

She grimaced at the dig. "Look, can we start over? We both came in with our own prejudices. Hard not to when we've both been burned, right?"

I nodded slowly. "Suppose so."

"As for why we need your help, well, it's obvious—or should be. You have inside knowledge of the Troika. You're the only one who's met the key players and knows their habits and perhaps their weaknesses. I know you want to run far from here, but where will you go? The Troika control the entire country. There's no place to hide, there's no normal life to return to. If you're going to survive, your only choice is to pick a side, dig in and fight. It's not a safe or a comfortable sort of life, but it's the best any of us can hope for right now. And maybe someday, if we keep fighting, we'll finally have a chance at safety and comfort again."

I sucked in a deep breath and released it slowly. Her words exposed my half-baked plan for the child's quest it had been. Children trusted wishes. Adults trusted facts. And the fact was I wouldn't last a week on my own. But I also might not survive three days if I stayed on to help.

"Look," she continued, "I understand the urge to lay down and just wait for death to take you." She unbuttoned her jacket. Peeking above the fabric of yellowed tank top she'd tattooed two red hearts. "But the way I look at it, if I'm going to die anyway, I might as well try to send as many of those bastards to hell as I can before I go. It won't bring them back." She placed a palm over the hearts. "But I'd rather die trying to destroy the Troika than to let death catch up to me because I couldn't run fast enough."

Her passion and anger reminded me of another strong female. One who took up arms against the Troika and inspired others to join her in the fight. One who would hold me in her lap while she made impassioned speeches to disheartened people about the importance of never losing hope. My eyes sought out the twin hearts on Dare's chest.

*Red means life.*

My mother had been talking about the red light of the Sisters of Crimson. But now I realized there were many meanings. Right then, it meant that the only path to freedom—to a real life— lay in spilling the Troika's blood.

"Well?" Dare said, her voice full of challenge. "What's it going to be?"

I sucked in a deep breath and held it, hoping the oxygen could dispel some of the fear. It didn't work, but at least my heart slowed a bit. Like it or not, I'd started this the moment I decided to run. In my hubris, I assumed I'd be able to outsmart my captors and manipulate the rebels to help me without having to get involved in the war. But once I'd seen the world outside the Troika's walls and saw the truth without Castor's propaganda-colored glasses, I knew I'd been a fool. The Chatelaine had been right—no one survived in this world without choosing a side. And since I could never choose the Troika, the process of elimination left the rebels.

I blew out the kind of deep breath one lets out just before they dive off a cliff. "Okay. I'm in."

Mom would have been so proud.

#

Two hours later, we all stood over Saga's map again. Icarus and Saga seemed to accept my change of heart like they'd expected it all along. Only Icarus seemed confused about the newfound respect between Dare and me. I could see in the looks he kept shooting at her that he wanted to know how she'd changed my mind. The blank stares she shot at him and the secret smile she tossed my way told me she'd keep my secrets safe. Whether out of feminine honor or just because she was mad at Icarus for electing her my executioner if I'd refused to help, I didn't know.

After the initial awkwardness when Dare and I had emerged, we got down to business. Rabbit sat nearby reading a book while the adults debated the plan.

"First we need to know who is most likely to be there," Dare said.

"Astyanax will be there," Saga said. "As head of the army and the Prime's personal guard, they'll want him there to oversee security."

The scent of brimstone and blood filled my nostrils as the scent memory of my last meeting with General Astyanax bullied its way in my brain. I shut down the memory of those weeks in the infirmary and focused on the mission.

"You can bet Castor will be there, too."

"But he's head of propaganda," Dare said. "Wouldn't they want to keep this quiet?"

I nodded. "Yes, but The Factory was his idea. He won't miss his moment of glory for anything."

"They need to know it was us," Icarus said suddenly. "Let Astyanax and Castor know that the rebels mean business."

I shook my head. "Absolutely not. You have to make it look like a mistake so they'll take it as a bad omen."

"Explain," Saga demanded.

"Castor is incredibly superstitious. You don't have to destroy the Factory. You just have to stage a convincing enough accident that Castor believes it's a bad sign. At a minimum, it will delay the project while he tries to figure out how to reverse the bad energy."

Icarus frowned. "There's no way we'll be able to get close enough to stage an accident with the General and his forces there."

Dare forced a derisive snort. "And if we get caught, the Troika will scramble to kill the camp prisoners faster in retaliation."

"Astyanax isn't as much of a threat as Castor," Saga said, almost to himself. "She's right, if we scare Castor we'll gain the advantage."

Dare and Icarus frowned at his dismissal of their concerns. "How can you say that, old man? Astyanax is the fiercest vampire alive."

Saga waved a hand to indicate the millions of books bearing witness to this dangerous meeting. "Because he who controls the information, rules the world. No weapon possessed by the Prime's army is more destructive than a single word from Castor's lying mouth."

"You'll never get to him, either," Dare said, turning away.

"It won't be easy," I said. "But it is possible. Castor is smart, but he's also got weaknesses."

"Like?" Saga asked, leaning forward.

"His ego, for one. He believes himself to be invincible. But he's also incredibly superstitious. I know for a fact that he's terrified of crossing the Sisters of Crimson."

"Why?"

I shrugged. "I have no idea, but he goes to church every Friday."

Dare looked up quickly. "Really?"

I nodded. Our eyes met for a brief moment. "There's a special chapel for upper-level Troika in the city. Its location isn't made public for security reasons, but I've been there."

"Why would they take you there if it's so secret?" Icarus sneered.

"Because when you're seen as nothing more than a blood dispenser," I tossed his words back at him, "no one believes you're capable of remembering anything important. If you want the biggest bang for your buck, go after The Factory. Make them believe their gods have damned their actions. It'll rattle their cages."

Saga rubbed his chin for a moment and eyed the map. "If we want to make a statement that will scare the Troika, we need to go big." Everyone stopped and stared, waiting for him to continue. Rabbit looked up and even Polonius tilted his head. Saga smiled and addressed us as one. "We've got to blow up the entire damned thing."

# SEVEN.

The Factory loomed in the distance— a slumbering metal giant. The cold, blue steel of the place set against the harsh light of the full moon sent a shiver down my spine. Train tracks webbed out from the complex, creating silvery moonlit traces.

Air steamed out of my mouth creating billowy white clouds against the blue night. On either side of me Dare, Rabbit and Icarus shivered in their shirt sleeves. "You're sure Castor will be here?" Icarus demanded, keeping his eyes trained on The Factory.

"The last time I saw him he was discussing this meeting. He said it had to be tonight because it's auspicious to begin new endeavors on the Feast of the Blood Moon." The Sanguinary Church celebration of the Feast of the Blood Moon was the vampire church's New Year, and Castor had decided to add mass murder to his list of resolutions.

Before we could discuss the matter further, a grinding noise echoed through the valley. We all jerked from surprise. Three warning alerts sounded from sirens posted along the rooftop.

"It's starting," Icarus said grimly.

Several windows lit up with bright orange and red light as the incinerators roared to life. A few moments later, white smoke belched from the thick chimneys that jutted from the roof like volcanoes.

Dare whispered, "They've woken the dragon."

A shudder passed through me and I swallowed the sudden knot of fear. This was suddenly all too, too real. When I'd told them about The Factory, I'd just been talking fast enough to save my life. But now, in the harsh cold of night with that monster breathing fire in the moonlight, I was paying the debts incurred by my quick tongue. Blowing up The Factory was one thing. Doing it with the head of the Troika's propaganda machine inside and his entire army surrounding the complex was a suicide mission.

"Steady," Dare whispered to me.

I jerked my gaze toward her. Before I could respond, movement to my right caught my attention. Rabbit was backing away, shaking his head. "I—I," he stuttered, face pale.

"Stop." Icarus commanded.

My vision filled with scarred Icarus in the foreground and the fires of the Troika's death machine burning in the background. Rabbit's head shook back and forth. I couldn't blame the kid for his fear. Icarus wanted that child to run toward Castor and his dragon, but anyone with an ounce of self-preservation would have run and kept running.

The kid stumbled on a rock. "Rabbit," Dare said, lurching forward. But Icarus shot her a look to stay out of it.

"I ran once, too." His quiet admission stilled my feet. He nodded. "During the battle of New York."

My eyes flared. "You were there?"

He nodded but kept his eyes on the kid. "I was twelve. Old enough to hold a gun, my father said. Old enough to fight."

I swallowed hard, remembering the chaos of those horrible days. The hunger and the noise and the smell of decay.

"Mom had died months earlier from an infection in her lungs. Dad tried real hard to teach me how to be brave in a fight. We sparred all the time and he made me practice shooting until I could hit a bull's eye every time." He licked his lips. "But all that training? It wasn't anything like the battle." His eyes went soft focus like he was watching a horror film in his head. Finally, he shook himself. "When dad got shot, it ... broke me. I'd been so gung ho to kill as many vamps as

I could until the moment I saw the red of my father's blood on my own skin. He kind of slumped over and I just snapped. Before I knew what I was doing, I was running as fast as I could without looking back. It wasn't until a few blocks later that I caught back up with myself. I still had the gun but I'd left my father's body behind in a gutter." His voice thickened with remorse.

I blinked quickly to clear the stinging. Rabbit was frozen, entranced by the story.

"I threw up twice before I gathered enough courage to go back. The battle had progressed and had taken over the block where I'd left him, so I had to be very careful. Luckily, I was pretty small for my age and could hide whenever a vampire patrol rolled past. It took me half an hour to get back the distance it had taken me five minutes to cover before."

Behind Icarus, Dare had gone quiet. Her expression was pained, like she couldn't decide whether this talk was what Rabbit needed or whether to protect him from the truth. I looked back at Rabbit and realized he was the same age as Icarus was in the story. Damn.

"When I got near the spot, a patrol had already found dad. I crouched behind a car and watched as one of the vampires nudged the body with a boot. It took everything I had not to rush out and attack that bastard for daring to disturb my father's dead body. But then the first scream reached me."

Rabbit squeezed his eyes closed.

"You see, my father hadn't died from the bullet."

My head started shaking to reject the horrors I knew were about to spill from his mouth. "Icarus—"

"Once they realized he was alive, they decided to play a little game."

"Stop," Dare whispered. "Please."

Rabbit's eyes opened wide as saucers. I wanted to punch Icarus for putting the kid through this. But then I realized that Rabbit didn't have the luxury of innocence. None of us did.

"First they stretched his body over the hood of a car. Then they took turns wounding him in increasingly elaborate and creative ways. By the time I came roaring from my hiding place, they'd ripped out one eye and peppered his arms and legs with more bullet holes and bite marks." His voice had taken on an edge of steel. "I managed to put a bullet through my father's brain and kill the bastard who took his eye before they took me down. If a superior officer hadn't come by and stopped them they would have done the same thing to me before they killed me. You see, dad was old and wounded, so he didn't matter. But me? I was strong and young, and the officer said the Troika would need slaves to build their empire once the war was over." He pointed a finger toward The Factory. "So yeah, I understand the need to run, but I also learned the hard way the price for my selfishness. If we don't stand up for our own, who will, Rabbit?"

Rabbit looked at Icarus with eyes older than they'd been ten minutes earlier. "But if we die, who will be left to fight?"

"If we don't fight, we might as well be dead."

Rabbit's Adam's apple bobbed convulsively in his throat. A shudder wracked his body, but he gathered himself together and stood straight. "Okay. Let's go."

"You sure, kiddo?" Dare asked.

Rabbit looked at her with an expression I hadn't seen from his innocent face before. Rebellion mixed with resentment over her insistence for treating him like a kid. "I'm fine," he snapped.

She quickly tamped the wounded look and nodded. "Let's do this."

Icarus smiled at the pair and then looked at me. "Well?"

I nodded, suddenly soul-tired. "Let's get it over with."

# EIGHT.

**D**own near the water, the air was colder and damp. The kind of cold that grabbed onto your bones with skeletal fingers.

Icarus waved us toward a dark mouth jutting over the river. Closer, I realized it was a drainage pipe. "All right. Those incinerators need an external fuel source. Most likely they've got massive propane tanks nearby with pipes leading underground into the Factory." He pointed toward a large, lone building about a hundred feet from the fence. Three guards in Troika uniforms stood out front with large guns. "There."

"Assuming we could get past them," I said, "what's the plan?"

Icarus removed something from his backpack. "We only have one chance with this." I squinted through the dark and saw a black device with a mess of wires and some sort of putty on the back. "If we can set this off on near the tanks, it'll cause a chain reaction through the pipes and destroy all the furnaces. The trick is to get in and out undetected so they believe it was a malfunction instead of an act of aggression. We can't risk the Troika retaliating against the people in the blood camps."

When we'd come up with this plan with Saga I'd argued that we needed way more than the four of us to pull it off. But it had taken us two days of walking to reach The Factory, and it would have taken three times that to contact another patrol group. Even longer for them to rendezvous with us. So Icarus wasn't kidding when he said we had one chance. If any of us were captured this plan was toast.

"I'll do it," Dare said.

Icarus shook his head. "The only way in is through this pipe. You won't fit." He was right. The pipe was narrower than the expanse of an average adult's shoulders.

My eyes swiveled toward the twelve-year-old child to my left. Dare's face went ghost pale. "Icarus, no—"

Rabbit ignored her and perked up. "I get to do it?"

Dare grabbed Icarus's arm and dragged him away. Rabbit cringed, like his mom and dad were fighting, and looked at me. "She treats me like a baby."

“She cares about you. That's a good thing."

He shrugged. "Sometimes she cares too much."

I wanted to lecture him and tell him to thank God that someone gave a shit about him. I wasn't under any illusions that Rabbit's life had been easy, but at least he never knew the soul crushing loneliness of having no one to depend on but himself. "Are you sure you're up for this?"

The instant I said it, I regretted the question. No doubt he'd see it as a challenge.

His chin came up. "Damn straight."

The cold night breeze carried Dare's raised voice toward us. Icarus's quieter responses were swallowed, but soon enough they both came to join us again. Icarus looked resigned and Dare looked defeated.

"All right, Rabbit, you're going to shimmy through the pipe. It'll lead you to a grate inside the compound. You'll have to sneak out of the pipe and get into that building." He took a few moments to show the kid how to engage the bomb. "Set the timer to two minutes from the time you engage it. That will give you a little lead time to get as far from the building as possible before it blows."

Rabbit practically pranced with excitement as he listened to the instructions. Dare hung back, staring off toward the river in the distance. Further downstream, the lights of Nachstadt created a surreal glow on the horizon. "You okay?" I asked, moving closer.

She shook herself and dragged her eyes from the lights. "I smell death on the air."

"Hopefully Troika deaths."

She just looked at me without speaking.

"Dare, Six?" Icarus called back. "He's ready."

Dare sighed and dragged herself out of whatever headspace she'd retreated to. "The master calls."

I looked up at the dim stars that were determined to be seen despite the city's lights and the Factory's fires. "Please." I wasn't sure to whom I was pleading or even what exactly I was asking for. I just knew that if anyone in the entire world needed help at that moment it was us.

#

Rabbit hung outside the tunnel long enough for us to take positions on a nearby rise. We needed to have a bird's eye view of the compound so we could warn him if any guards were close. Icarus held a small remote in his hand. A punch of the button would set off a small shock on a sensor around Rabbit's wrist. It wasn't the best warning system, but it was all we had. Besides, even if we'd had a more sophisticated verbal warning system, we couldn't have risked interference getting picked up by the guards' walkie-talkies.

Once we were in position, Icarus sent a quick double-zap to the kid to let him know it was time to go. We were far enough away that Rabbit looked incredibly small and very young beside the dark river and the pipe's wide mouth. An instant after Icarus hit the button, the kid looked down at his wrist and then waved to signal he'd received the message.

Dare let out a long, nervous breath. I shot her a look that I hoped was reassuring despite my own nerves. Were we really sending that kid into a heavily fortified compound alone? The list of things that could go wrong was so long, it was laughable.

"There he goes," Icarus whispered. We all tensed as Rabbit's wingtips disappeared into the hole.

Dare raised her binoculars. "The guards do a lap around the building every two minutes. If he can time it right, he'll be able to enter the outbuilding through the window in the back between rounds."

"The trick will be getting out of range before the explosion goes," Icarus said in a grave tone.

When she responded, Dare didn't lower the binoculars. "If he dies, I'm holding you responsible."

"If he dies, we all will," Icarus shot back. "Either from the bomb or when the guards find us."

We all fell silent then. The minutes ticked by like years. The orange light from the furnaces lit up the compound like the fires of hell. Figures in black Troika uniforms swarmed the perimeter and the buildings. And my heart thumped in my ears like war drums.

"There he is," Dare whispered, pointing. I grabbed the binoculars from her. Sure enough, a small head was peeking out from a grate not twenty feet from the outbuilding. I held my breath as the mop of hair rose a little higher and his eyes appeared to scan the area.

But before he could gather his courage and climb out of his hiding place, a commotion near the compound grabbed our attention. The wind whipped up and landing lights flashed to announce the arrival of a transport rover bearing the Troika's official seal.

"Damn it." Icarus raised his voice over the high-pitched whine of the rover's engine. He punched the button to indicate Rabbit should stay put. The rover landed in the center of the compound and was quickly surrounded by every guard in the vicinity.

"Hold on," Dare said. "Look." She pointed to the outbuilding, where two of the guards ran from their post to join those surrounding the rover. That left only one guard at the front and the back completely unguarded.

Icarus checked to be sure no guards were approaching the area around Rabbit's grate. When the coast was clear, he punched the button twice. A couple of seconds later, Rabbit burst out of his hidey hole and ran as fast as his skinny legs would carry him toward the window at the back of the building. My heart pounded in time with his footsteps. "Come on, kid."

Rabbit reached the back wall of the building and paused. From my vantage point, I could see his bird-thin chest heaving from the exertion. His head swiveled from side to side, looking for any ambushes. I looked toward the rover and froze. Astyanax had already exited the craft and Castor was climbing out after him. The General was tall as a tree and built like a tank. Where the guards carried assault weapons, Astyanax carried no weapons other than his massive fangs, which protruded from his mouth like a saber tooth tiger's.

By comparison, Castor was smaller and more elegantly turned out. He wore a sleek black business suit and a blood red tie. His blond hair was slicked back and his too-red lips stood out lushly against his milk-white skin. Despite his refined appearance, I knew for a fact he had the eyes and the personality of a venomous snake. You never knew when he'd strike, but he always did. Once his feet hit *terra firma*, Castor spun around to admire his latest victory in his quest to become the top engineer of nightmares for humans. He spread his arms wide and laughed. His breath hit the chilly air and rose like smoke.

"Quickly," I urged. "If we can get the explosion to go off while they're taking their tour—"

"He's moving toward the window now."

Rabbit fumbled to remove the package from his shirt. Icarus was watching the guards while the kid worked. "Shit," he said. "The guards are going back to their posts now that Castor and Astyanax are going inside for their tour."

Sure enough one of the returning guards broke off and started his way around the building. "Get him out of there!" Dare shouted.

"He's almost done," Icarus argued. "A few more seconds."

"There's no time." She lunged for him and grabbed the remote. Taken by surprise, Icarus lost control of the device easily. She punched the button hard. Down in the compound, Rabbit jerked and looked around quickly. Seeing no one, he shook his head and returned to fumbling with the buttons on the device. Dare cursed and hit the button again. "C'mon, kid, run!"

In just a few more steps, the guard would reach the corner. Once he rounded it, he'd see Rabbit and all hell would break loose. Dare hit the button three times in quick succession. The kid must have finally gotten the message. He jumped away from the window and darted back in the direction of this grate and freedom.

The three of us jumped up from our crouches. "Run! Go, Rabbit!"

The kid was ten feet from freedom when the guard came around the corner.

He was only five feet away when the bullet hit him in the back.

# NINE.

Even if I lived to be a hundred, which was frankly looking less and less likely every second, I would never forget the moment when Rabbit fell. Time slowed like we were watching through water. We were so far away we couldn't hear the gun go off, but we saw the bloom of red an instant before the kid stumbled to his knees. I don't remember exactly what happened next, except that once time caught back up with the three of us, we were screaming. Dare had fallen to her knees and covered her ears with her hands. Icarus shouted "Rabbit!" and then fell ominously silent. I'm not exactly sure what I said, but I knew that my throat hurt and tears fell cold on my cheeks.

All of this happened in less than a minute. Then, down far below, a swarm of black surrounded the kid and blocked our view. My eyes searched the area, looking for something, any sign of hope. Somehow my gaze landed back on that window and the small black device still attached to the glass. I hit Icarus on the arm. "The bomb!"

He dragged his eyes from the vampires surrounding the kid and looked at me with red-rimmed eyes. "What?"

"They didn't find the bomb."

He shook himself, like a man waking up from a deep sleep and grabbed the binoculars from me. "Fuck me." He looked down at his watch. "It should have gone off by now."

Dare stood on the edge of the rise, staring at the mass of black figures. "He's alive," she whispered. She reached back and grabbed my sleeve. "He's alive!"

I stumbled forward and looked where she was pointing. The black uniforms had parted. One of the vampires pulled Rabbit up from the ground. At first, it appeared he wasn't responding, but, then, he got his feet under him and his head rolled back. I grabbed Icarus's binoculars. "Holy shit! She's right." The kid's eyes were open and his mouth was moving. I couldn't tell if he was screaming from pain or merely begging for his life. Regardless, he was alive. I rounded on Icarus. "We have to save him."

He stared hard at the unfolding drama far below. The guards were dragging Rabbit toward the center of the compound. No doubt they planned on taking him to Castor for instructions. If we could make the bomb go off before they decided on a course of action, we might have a chance for getting Rabbit away from the guards.

Finally, Icarus looked at Dare with sorrow. "It's too late for him."

She launched at him, punching at his chest and face with wild hands. "Fuck you! We're not leaving him!"

"Stop, Dare. Stop!" He struggled to get her flailing limbs under control. His scars were pale against his flushed skin. "Listen! Our only chance to save him is to set off the bomb. Stop!" He grabbed her by the upper arms and shook her. "If the bomb goes off he's dead anyway."

She stumbled back, sobbing. "We have to try!"

My chest felt like someone had bound my ribs with steel bands. Icarus looked at me for help. All I could think was that I would not let another child die by Troika hands. "That bomb has to go off no matter what. We need to get over that fence. You two go and wait for the first explosion and then grab the kid and run like hell."

Dare sniffed. "What about you? How will you get out?"

"We don't have time to argue about this. We need to get in and make this happen or we'll lose Rabbit and any chance to pull off this mission," I said. "If you make it out alive, we'll rendezvous down river, in the abandoned church."

With that, I turned my back on the pair before they could stop me. There was no other way this could play out. If I tried to save Rabbit and Castor saw me, he would stop at nothing to kill all of us. Better for him to believe this was a ragtag team of random rebels.

It took me a few minutes to make it to the fence. In that amount of time, the furor over capturing Rabbit still hadn't died down. The guards had done a quick sweep of the area round where he was captured, but finding nothing, decided to gather in clumps near the main building to watch Castor decide what to do with the kid. I tried to keep my eyes away from that area because I couldn't afford to be distracted by what they were doing to the kid. Losing my nerve now would sign all of our death warrants.

As I neared the fence, I listened for the tell-tale hum that indicated electricity. Even though it was silent, I still threw at small metal wrench at it to be sure. When it hit without causing a spark, I knew it was safe to climb. I should have been surprised the Troika hadn't bothered electrifying the fence, but they always underestimated what a group of determined rebels could accomplish. The metal fence was twelve feet high but the pillars were made from wood and stone, which gave me hand- and footholds and some semblance of cover until I got to the top.

I landed on the other side and crouched down to the balls of my feet. A quick glance around proved that the area was clear. Further into the compound, I could hear shouting and the sounds of running boots. But for now I was blessedly alone. The outbuilding that held the propane tanks was fifty feet from the fence. I ran there full-tilt and reached the back of the building in no time.

The black box was still attached to the bottom of the window. A quick peek inside made my stomach drop and a whispered curse escape my lips. A handful of guards were inspecting the tanks. Probably they were worried Rabbit had tried to sabotage them from inside the building. I ducked down so my head was below the window. Looking up, I studied the face of the device to figure out what had gone wrong. A green light flashed on the front, but the count-down timer wasn't engaged. I realized that in his rush, Rabbit had forgotten to flip the final switch. Chewing my bottom lip, I adjusted the function of the timer so it gave us five minutes, instead of two, before it exploded. Then, I held my breath, sent a prayer to a God I didn't believe in, and clicked on the switch that engaged the count down. Red numbers flashed up 5:00. Once I made sure it flipped over to 4:59, I took off running.

And ran straight into a chest wearing a black uniform.

My adrenaline spiked and lightning zinged under my sweaty skin. Luckily, he was as surprised as I was by our collision. Unlucky for him, I recovered first and grabbed his gun from his holster. I slammed the metal into his temple and pulled the trigger. His eyes widened and a gasp escaped his mouth. In the next instant, he slumped in to me. I let him fall to the ground and ran. The gun's weight was reassuring in my hand. I started for the fence again, but a female scream reached my ears.

Dare.

Fuck. I swiveled and hauled ass across the compound, shooting any guard I ran into along the way. The gunfire drew more and more guards, but I didn't care. If I didn't get myself and my team out of there in the next three minutes we'd all be dead anyway.

I broke into the clearing at a dead run. The heat from the furnaces radiated off the building like a sun. Sweat covered every inch of skin and my heart pounded depth charges in my chest. In the center of the clearing, Dare knelt on the ground next to Rabbit's still form. Meanwhile Icarus stood defiant before Castor despite the dozens of gun aimed at him. I didn't slow my pace. Just ran toward them like a wild woman, screaming. The guards turned to see what the commotion was about and when they saw me their mouths fell open.

I was almost to Castor and his prisoners when a very large body stepped in my path. I skidded to a stopped mere inches from Astyanax. He loomed above me like a colossus. His fangs flashed in the light from the moon and the fires forming inside The Factory. My bowls went watery, but I raised the gun.

A massive fist swiped the weapon away with little effort. His other hand swung around and made contact with my jaw. I fell back as Castor started laughing.

"Meridian Six," Castor drawled. He held a hand up to forestall Astyanax's advance. "Why am I not surprised to find you in league with this pathetic group of weaklings."

I spit a mouthful of blood at his feet. "Let us go or I'll set off the bomb I just installed on your propane stores." I held up the remote we'd used earlier to warn Rabbit. Castor bought the lie and stilled.

"What are your demands?" His tone was too casual. He was coiling like a snake preparing to strike.

"Let the boy go," I said, looking him directly in his yellow eyes. "The other two, as well."

Castor's eyebrows rose up. "That's all?"

I shook the remote in the air. "We'll see."

The corner of his red lips lifted. "Never try to bluff a professional liar, Six." He nodded toward Astyanax. I felt the air shift as the general moved toward me. In slow motion, I pivoted and held up an arm to ward off the fangs. But in the next instant, the deafening boom of an explosion blew across the clearing like a hurricane of fire, bringing with it searing heat and a concussion like a punch to the diaphragm.

The impact knocked me off my feet and sent my body flying toward the spot where Icarus had stood a moment earlier. A high-pitched whine filled my ears and my eyes stung and were wet. I swiped at them and my hand came away bloody. Despite the pain and confusion, a single thought screamed inside my head: RUN!

The chain reaction hadn't spread through the Factory's pipeline. But it was coming. If I didn't get us out of there *now* we were going to burn. Even though my eyes hurt like hellfire, I squinted through the smoke and located Icarus a couple of feet away. I groped toward him. "Icarus! Can you hear me?" I couldn't hear myself, but judging from the way my throat ached, I was screaming. He rolled over and blinked once, twice, three times before he jerked into motion.

"Dare? Rabbit?" he mouthed.

"There!" Dare was lying on top of Rabbit over near a wheel of the rover. Together, Icarus and I leaned into each other, supporting each other's weights. We stumbled to the ground by Dare and pulled her off him. A trickle of blood glared red beneath her left ear and her eyes were shot through with broken capillaries.

Icarus grabbed her off the ground, supporting all of her weight when she didn't do it on her own. He jerked his head toward Rabbit. I leapt toward the kid and hauled him up to my shoulder with strength borne from fear and adrenaline.

When I turned to follow Icarus, I saw Astyanax's smoldering body nearby. His large body had taken most of the brunt of the explosion and it showed. A quick look around revealed dozens of other burning bodies, but I didn't detect Castor's among the injured.

Shaking myself, I sped up to follow Icarus onto the open door of the rover. I prayed he knew how to fly it because we didn't have time for a tutorial. The ground was shaking as explosions occurred in the pipeline underground.

I lay Rabbit on one of the plush benches inside the rover and went to hit the button to seal us in. The sound of the engines whirring to life filled the cabin. Icarus had dumped a shell-shocked Dare into the co-pilot's seat and taken the throttle. "Hold on!" he yelled.

The world tilted wildly. I grabbed onto a handle and held on with white knuckles. As the earth fell away below us, it felt like I'd left my stomach behind. Through the front window I could see the stars getting closer, which meant we were getting farther from The Factory. The last ten minutes had felt like an eternity.

"Shit, Six." Icarus's warning came a split second before The Factory went boom. The concussion rocked the rover, causing it to dip and stutter in mid-air. A sensor started beeping furiously.

"Hang on!" Icarus yelled. He didn't have to tell me twice. I braced my feet and grabbed onto handholds on the ceiling.

Finally stable, I turned to look out of the rear window of the rover. Where The Factory had stood now looked like the mouth of hell. We'd done it. We'd destroyed the Troika's dragon before it could consume any humans.

The sensor stopped beeping and the rover's altitude leveled off. For a moment, I allowed myself to just breath easy.

Rabbit groaned from the bench. My short-lived respite over—I moved to check on him. The bullet had gone straight through his shoulder. Not a lethal wound, but blood loss could pose a major problem. His skin was pale and clammy, and his mouth worked like he wanted to scream, but he didn't open his eyes.

"How is he?" Icarus called.

"Alive, but he needs medical attention."

Before Icarus could answer, the door to the rover's electrical closet burst open.

Castor launched at me looking like something straight out of hell. His once-elegant face was bloody and patches of skin were charred beyond recognition. I fell back into the bench where Rabbit lay as Castor's weight slammed into me. His fangs snapped like a beast's toward my neck. To heal his wounds, he'd need an infusion of blood. My blood.

"Icarus!" I screamed. But I knew he couldn't help me. Someone had to fly the rover.

"The Prime should have killed you when your

brat turned out to be a low blood!" he snarled.

I fought and scratched at the vampire's face. I kicked with heavy, sore legs. I screamed my rage at his horrific, burned face.

Movement from my peripheral vision. Then Castor's weight lifted off me. Dare had shaken off her shock and come to the rescue. She and Castor faced off. Her yellow eyes flashed and she hissed, flashing those empty fang sockets. Despite being a eunuch, she looked every inch the fearsome predator capable of murder.

"Six!" she snarled. "The door."

I lunged at the wall and punched the button. The door slid open. Air wooshed in like a cyclone, whipping my hair around and pulling my body toward the opening. I grabbed a seatbelt from a nearby bench and held on.

Dare shoved Castor with every ounce of strength she had. The male vampire stumbled back toward the door. He fell back against the benches along that wall. He was up again in a blink. Knowing Dare was the stronger foe, he lunged for me this time. But just as his clawed hands snagged my shirt, the necklace the Chatelaine gave me sprang from the neckline. One of his hands brushed against the red disk. He hissed and pulled away as if he'd been burned.

"Where did you get that?"

Confusion held me frozen. Before I could answer, Dare ran and flew at his midsection with a kick.

Castor's eyes went wide. His hands windmilled wildly and then the air current took hold of his body and sucked him through the door. His screams were swallowed by the wind.

Before any thoughts of celebrating the death of Castor could sink in, Dare's body flew toward the opening. I grabbed her arm just before her body was vacuumed into the night, as well. With one hand holding on to the seat belt and the other wrapped around her wrist, I struggled with every ounce of strength in my body to reel her back inside. But my hands were sweaty and my strength was gone. She was starting to slip away.

I screamed from exertion and frustration. Her eyes were wide and she scrambled to hold on. I was losing her.

A warm arm wrapped around my waist and a hand appeared to grab Dare's wrist next to mine. I looked up to see Icarus's grim face as he pulled both of us out of harm's way. I fell back onto the bench. Sure that Icarus had Dare safely inside, I slapped a palm on the button to slam the door shut.

The silence that followed was punctuated with gasps and curses. I looked at Dare's wild hair and her trembling body, and at Icarus's dirt-streaked and scarred face. "The rover?" I asked.

"Auto-pilot. We'll land in the Badlands and ditch it. We can't go back to Book Mountain, but maybe Jeremiah and his squad will take us in."

"They'll have us," Dare said. "We have

Meridian Six on our team."

I frowned at her. "What's that supposed to mean?"

"Don't you get it?" Icarus said. "The daughter of Alexis Sargosa is finally on the rebel's side and she's declared war against the Troika."

My mouth fell open. "That's not what happened—"

Icarus laughed humorlessly. “Doesn't matter. They'll believe what we tell them,” he said, sounding too much like the vampire we'd just killed for my comfort. “We'll have to start calling you Carmina, though. Meridian Six has too many bad associations.” He narrowed his eyes at me. I didn't like the speculative glint I saw there. “Carmina Sargosa,” he tested the words on his tongue. “Yes. It's got a noble air to it. The kind of name people rally around. A leader.”

I looked over toward Rabbit, who lay watching us. His skin was pale and his eyes were feverish, but he was alive. I moved toward him and cradled his small body, careful not to hurt his wounds too much. I pretended I was trying to comfort him, but I needed it, too. Icarus's words had left me feeling both hollow and dirty, used. He didn't want me to be a leader. He wanted me to be his puppet.

How could I have been so naïve to think I could start a new life on my own terms? Hadn't I already learned that the world was made up of two types: The Users and The Used. I'd tried to use the rebels to earn my freedom, but I'd ended up being a pawn. Again.

Sure, I wanted the Troika to pay for everything it had taken from me, everything it had withheld. In that sense I guess I was on the rebels' side. But listening to Icarus speak, an icy hand skittered up my spine. I'd let myself get carried away kicking the hornets' nest and I was pretty sure before this was all over, I'd be the one to feel the Troika's sting. "What have I done?" I whispered, mostly to myself.

Icarus smiled that smile that transformed his ravaged face. Only this time it scared me. "You just gave us the weapon we need to defeat the Troika."

I frowned at him. "What kind of weapon?"

"The same one that's been at the center of every good revolution." He tilted his head. "A good story to inspire the troops."

With that, he rose to check on the cockpit again. Dare nudged me out of the way to get to the kid. I dropped onto a bench across the way.

Through the side window, the stars were laid out like a blanket of diamonds. At that altitude it was easy to forget all the destruction and violence, the hopelessness so common on the ground. Up there it was easy to imagine a future where Rabbit could grow up healthy and happy. One where I was able to live on my own terms without someone wanting to use me for their cause.

I looked down at the red lotus totem Sister Agrippa had given me. The one that was a symbol of her faith. Faith that terrified Castor so much it cost him his life. I squeezed my hand around the red disk until it bit into the palm. Maybe it was time for me to have a little faith, too.

Through the rover's cockpit and toward the horizon, I saw another sign of hope. While behind us The Factory still burned like Hephaestus's forge, up ahead another fire glowed, one far more dangerous to the Troika than any man-made inferno. Dawn streaked across the lavender sky in a fury of orange, yellow and red, announcing the sun's imminent arrival.

The sun was the enemy of every vampire—a fire demon. But I was a human, and to my kind the sun was an angel of life. It nourished our crops and our livestock. It warmed our skin and helped us see. It provided us with energy and a reason to rise every morning.

I closed my eyes and imagined absorbing its heat into my pores and filling up my chest cavity with its awesome power.

My name was Carmina Sargosa, daughter of Alexis Sargosa. And like the sun, I would rise above the Troika and finish the work my mother began. I would burn every last vampire to the ground.

*Red means life.*

# ABOUT THE AUTHOR

Jaye Wells is a USA Today-bestselling author of urban fantasy and speculative crime fiction. Raised by booksellers, she loved reading books from a very young age. That gateway drug eventually led to a full-blown writing addiction. When she's not chasing the word dragon, she loves to travel, drink good bourbon and do things that scare her so she can put them in her books. Jaye lives in Texas.

Connect with me online:
Twitter: http://twitter.com/JayeWells
Facebook: https://www.facebook.com/AuthorJayeWells
Web site: http://www.JayeWells.com

Printed in Poland
by Amazon Fulfillment
Poland Sp. z o.o., Wrocław